The Beastly Earl and his Rose

VIOLET SINCLAIR

Copyright © [Year of First Publication] by [Author or Pen Name]

All rights reserved.

No portion of this book may be reproduced in any form without written permission from the publisher or author, except as permitted by U.S. copyright law.

Contents

1. Chapter One — 1
2. Chapter Two — 11
3. Chapter Three — 17
4. Chapter Four — 27
5. Chapter Five — 37
6. Chapter Six — 47
7. Chapter Seven — 55
8. Chapter Eight — 69
9. Chapter Nine — 83
10. Chapter Ten — 99
11. Chapter Eleven — 107
12. Chapter Twelve — 117
13. Chapter Thirteen — 127
14. Chapter Fourteen — 139

15.	Chapter Fifteen	145
16.	Chapter Sixteen	157
17.	Chapter Seventeen	163
18.	Chapter Eighteen	181
19.	Chapter Nineteen	189
20.	Chapter Twenty	199
21.	Chapter Twenty-One	213
22.	Epilogue	221
About Violet Sinclair		225
Also by Violet Sinclair		227
Seductive Secrets and Regency Romance		243

Chapter One

Leicester, England 1817

It wasn't like she was one of those frivolous ladies who pranced around indulging in swooning fits. No, Miss Rose Sheffield had always looked down upon those types and vowed to never become one. However, recent events had her questioning her resolve. Perhaps a slight fainting spell wouldn't harm her lofty morals, she mused while giving the butler a stern look as he stood in her way. But just as quickly, she brushed off the thought with frustration.

"What do you mean her ladyship is not present?" She raised her black veil to get a better look at the old man standing before her. "I specifically wrote my great-aunt that I was coming!"

"I am quite sure you did, Miss Sheffield, correct?" the head butler said, his tone dripping with condescension as he scrutinized her from head to toe. "However, if you did send a letter, it seems to have been misplaced. And I do not recall the countess mentioning any expected guests, as she surely would have. Perhaps you have the incorrect address?" He finished with a smug smile that made Rose's blood boil.

She briefly considered the satisfaction that would come from striking the butler's balding head with her reticule, but she was too exhausted to even try. The journey from her London residence, which should have taken two days, dragged on for four instead. She was at her wit's end. First, her rented carriage broke down and lost a wheel. Then one of the horses became lame. And just to add insult to injury, the drunken driver she hired managed to take them in the wrong direction.

She was utterly drained, her body sore from the relentless jostling. All she yearned for was to collapse onto a featherbed and slumber for days on end. Alas, it appeared that even such modest indulgences would be denied by a fickle destiny. Suppressing the urge to succumb to fainting spells, she lifted her head and locked eyes with the butler's distrustful stare

"May I inquire as to Lady Howe's whereabouts? I have a note that simply cannot wait," she huffed, desperately trying to maintain her facade of calmness.

The butler paused, then replied, "Lady Howe is currently in Scotland attending the arrival of her grandchild. As for her return, it is anyone's guess."

"She has gone to Aberdeen?" Rose exclaimed in dismay, the hope that her aunt was enjoying a mere weekend in the country vanishing.

The fact that Rose knew her ladyship's oldest son lived in Aberdeen seemed to relieve the elder butler of some of his reservations, although he still showed a marked reluctance to let Rose inside.

The gentleman's tone was now less condescending as he replied, "Miss Sheffield, the lady is currently residing with the earl and his wife at St. Andrew's Square. If you desire, I can pass along your message for you. And are you planning to stay in Leicester?" Rose could infer from this that staying in the grand manor house was not a possibility, and she held back her frustration. "If you could recommend a reputable inn, I will be lodging there," she responded, already considering the difficulties of being an unescorted woman at a public inn. She had hired a companion to accompany her from London, but convincing the older woman to remain indefinitely may prove challenging.

"The Crooked Crow is all the rage among the fashionable set, my dear. I'm sure you'll find it quite suitable," the butler stammered, clearly at a loss for what to do. "If Lady Harriet had left any instructions for your stay here, I would gladly oblige, but alas…" His voice trailed off as he shrugged helplessly.

Rose sensed his wavering, and considered pressing her advantage. But in the end, she deemed it not worth the effort and accepted defeat with a tired sigh. "That's quite alright. I understand you can't let me in without permission," she said, suppressing the urge to scheme her way past him.

"If you need anything, I'll send a maid to attend to you," the butler offered eagerly. "It wouldn't do for a member of the countess's family to be waited on by an inn's common maid."

Whereas it would apparently "do" for a member of her ladyship's family to stay at that same inn, Rose thought with a flash of her usual irreverence. "That is not necessary, sir. I brought my own maid with me." She raised her chin to give the man a mocking smile. "But I do thank you for the kind offer," she added, her tone fairly dripping with sarcasm. She then turned and stalked back to the waiting carriage.

"Well, what is it?" her companion, Mrs. Nettles demanded, her black eyes full of distrust as Rose climbed inside. "Your great-aunt refuse to see you? I'm not surprised; you likely offended her sensibilities by arriving in a rented hack. The gentry's queer that way, did I not warn you?"

"Oh, but of course you did, Mrs. Nettles, at least a dozen times," Rose scoffed with a dramatic eye roll. She leaned back against the luxurious velvet cushions and let out an exaggerated sigh, feeling as if she had been trapped for an eternity in that cramped carriage with the older woman's strict manners and acidic tongue. Rose did not know what she feared more—the older woman with her rigid sensibilities and a tongue that dripped acid would refuse to stay with another day, or that she would agree.

"What is amiss?" Mrs. Nettles propped, her brows meeting gin a scowl. "If your aunt isn't refusing you the door, why are you still here? We're not lost again, are we?"

Rose's temper flared as she bit back her retort. "We are not lost, nor has my aunt denied me entry," she forced out through clenched teeth.

"It seems her ladyship has gone to Aberdeen for a visit, and since she left no instructions to the contrary, the staff cannot let me stay in the house. We shall have to ut up at an inn until I contact my aunt."

"We?" Mrs. Nettles' expression grew even more sour.

Rose clenched her hands in her lap, trying to maintain composure in the face of Mrs. Nettles' haughty judgement. "I was hoping you would be so kind as to stay with me," she said through gritted teeth, inwardly fuming at the social norms that required such an arrangement. "Maggie is here with me, but it would be better for appearances if I had a proper chaperone."

"I would certainly hope so," Mrs. Nettles sniffed loudly, casting a disdainful glance at the middle-aged maid sitting beside Rose. "It is scandalous enough for an unmarried woman to stay at an inn, let alone with only a lowly maid as company..." She shuddered in disgust at the thought. "Well, I am sure I need not tell you what people would think about that."

Arrogant old hag, Rose thought with a controlled expression. "So, you will be staying then?" Mrs. Nettles stiffened her posture. "As a Christian woman, I am well aware of my duties, Miss Sheffield. I would never abandon a fellow sister in peril or risk damaging her reputation. You have my word that I will stay for as long as needed."

With that hurdle behind her, Rose was able to scrape up a tired smile. "than you , Ma'am. That is most gracious of you."

"Of course, " the other woman added, a sly look in her dark eyes, "I was paid to accompany you only as far as Leicester. I had planned to return home on the next mail coach, as I have another position waiting for me. But naturally I shan't give such paltry financial considerations another thought."

perhaps she wouldn't be internally damned if she would accidentally kick the old witch's shins, Rose thought, wistfully studying Mrs. Nettles's bombazine-draped limbs. She had but to uncross her ankles and...

"I should be more than happy to reimburse you the inconvenience, Mrs. nettles," she said instead, mentally admonishing herself for the lapse in control. "Another ten pounds, shall we say?"

"I would have made fifteen at the other post." Mrs. Nettles' prompt reply told Rose she had been unwisely generous in her initial offer.

"Fifteen, then," Rose agreed, than uncrossed her ankles, allowing the toe of her kid half-boots to come into painful contact with Mrs. Nettles' thick ankles.

"Ouch!"

"Did I kick you?" Rose's eyes were wide with innocence. "Oh dear, how very clumsy of me. I am sorry."

"Cantankerous, ill-tempered, money-grubbing old hag!" Maggie muttered, her voice thick with frustration as she tossed Rose's belongings into the small wardrobe with a fury that matched her words.

"Honestly, I've never known anyone who could teach vinegar how to be bitter! Why in heaven's name did you hire her? It must've been a moment of lunacy, I swear."

"Please, Maggie, no more," Rose groaned, pressing the lavender-soaked cloth against her aching temples. "My head feels as though it's splitting apart."

"And little wonder!" Maggie lowered her voice but her annoyance simmered just beneath the surface. "Four days with that woman would drive a saint to madness. And as for you—well, your father would've thought you'd taken leave of your senses, letting her walk all over you like that."

Rose cracked open one eye, shooting her maid a glare. "I? I have been the very picture of propriety!"

Maggie crossed her arms, leveling Rose with an accusing stare. "Exactly. Since when have you ever been a simpering miss, taking that woman's nonsense without a single sharp retort? I could hardly believe my eyes, watching you behave like some green girl fresh from the schoolroom."

"I wasn't simpering!" Rose snapped, her pride bruised at the mere suggestion.

"And you certainly weren't putting Mrs. Nettles in her place, either!" Maggie was relentless. "Whatever's come over you? You've never been one to play the ninnyhammer before."

Rose's irritation faltered under the weight of Maggie's honest bewilderment. The maid had known her since she was in short frocks, after all. With a weary sigh, Rose collapsed back onto the bed, the springs creaking beneath her. Silence stretched between them as she struggled to find words to explain the change that had crept up on her.

"Maybe," she whispered at last, her eyes clouded with doubt, "maybe I'm just tired of playing the vixen. Of being the one who always fights back." Her hands clenched in her lap as she stared at them. "Maybe it's my fault Papa disinherited me. If I hadn't been so willful, so stubborn... perhaps he wouldn't have felt the need to cut me off."

Maggie's eyes widened in shock. "But your father was always disinheriting you! Why, he cut you out of his will at least three times a year, only to put you back in once his temper cooled. Even Mr. Pembroke, his solicitor, said he was sure it was just another fit of pique."

"Except this time, he died before he could undo it," Rose whispered, her voice tight with regret. "Maybe... if I hadn't quarreled with him so much, he wouldn't have felt the need to disinherit me at all."

"Now that's just nonsense, and you know it." Maggie shook her head, disbelief etched on her face. "You think you failed him? He loved you more than anything, Rose. He'd have moved heaven and earth for you."

Rose blinked, tears stinging her eyes. "I loved him too, Maggie. But he wanted me to be someone I wasn't. Someone quiet, obedient. A daughter who knew her place, who didn't argue or fight. Instead, he got me."

Maggie hurried over, sitting beside her on the bed and grasping her hands tightly. "Oh, pet. Don't say that. Your father was as proud as could be of you. Why, I can't count the times he'd laugh and say, 'That daughter of mine would walk into Hades and have the devil running for his life.' Does that sound like a man who regretted you?"

Secretly, Rose wasn't so sure. Her father had said those words to her too, but now they rang hollow. In his final days, he had urged her to accept Ronald's proposal, insisting that it was time she settled down, time she stopped being so "unfeminine." At the time, she had thought he was simply testing her resolve. Now she wasn't so certain.

Maggie gave her hand a firm squeeze, breaking through her thoughts. "It's your nerves talking, that's what. After everything you've been through—the sudden loss of your father, the court battle over the will... well, it's no wonder you're worn thin. But you'll see, with a little rest, you'll be back to your old self."

Rose swallowed the knot of emotion building in her throat. "I don't know if I want to be that person anymore, Maggie," she admitted softly. "I'm not sure I know who I am without the fight."

Maggie paused, her expression softening. "You're still you, Rose. And the person you are is stronger than you know. Rest now, pet. The fight can wait until tomorrow."

Rose dutifully closed her eyes, the gentle click of the door signaling Maggie's departure. But the moment she heard her footsteps fade, her eyes flew open again. My old self, she thought bitterly, rolling onto her side, staring at the cracked plaster ceiling. A fine lot of good that version of me ever did anyone.

She had bulldozed through life, embracing her every whim and wild fancy with little care for the consequences. Each quarrel with her father, every scandalous word or deed, had felt like a game. A game she'd once believed they both enjoyed equally—hadn't he been the one to tell her never to bow to any man? To always think for herself?

And yet, the cold whisper of doubt gnawed at her insides. If that were true, then why couldn't she shake this horrible sense that she'd failed him? Their last argument, sparked by her refusal to entertain her insipid cousin Ronald's yearly proposal, had been their most vicious yet. The memory of it still clung to her like a bruise that refused to fade.

Ronald had journeyed down from Nottingham on his annual visit, as predictably as the turning of the seasons, and as ever, he had proposed. She'd turned him down, as she always did, thinking that would be the end of it. But then her father, to her shock, had pressed the matter. The very thought of it made her stomach twist.

Marriage to Ronald, her father had mused, his eyes peering at her over his spectacles, might not be such a bad thing after all.

Rose had been appalled. "The man's a fop and a fool!" she'd exclaimed, her voice sharp enough to cut through the thick tension in the room.

Her father had sighed, rubbing a hand over his face. "The lad only needs guidance. And you, Rose, you've always enjoyed leading men around by the nose. The two of you might suit."

Rose had retorted with acid in her voice that the only thing Ronald could possibly want leading him was a tailor to outfit his next ridiculous ensemble. And just like that, the battle had begun. The more her father urged the match, the more obstinate she had become. His dramatic declaration of disinheriting her had followed soon after, and in retaliation, she'd threatened to run off and become a governess—a taunt meant to provoke him, not one she'd ever thought she might have to act on.

And then, three days later, he had died in his sleep, leaving her with words unspoken and wounds unhealed.

Rose shifted restlessly beneath the thin blanket, the memories pressing down on her chest. That was what hurt the most, the thought she had been carrying like a stone inside her. He had died thinking her a failure, disappointed in the sharp tongue and rebellious nature he himself had fostered in her. The last thing he'd said to her had stung more than any argument they'd ever had: For once in your life, I'd like to see you act like a lady should.

And now he was gone, forever, leaving her to wonder whether her pride—her willful, untamed spirit—had been worth the price.

No more, she vowed to herself, swiping at the tears that blurred her vision. She had tried being the stubborn shrew, the brazen woman who took pleasure in challenging the world. And look where it had landed her—disinherited, alone, and questioning every step she'd taken. From now on, she would be what her father had wanted. Demure. Well-behaved. Quiet, no matter the provocation. The perfect lady, exactly as he had wished.

The thought brought a strange sort of peace. She had already started, hadn't she? Mrs. Nettles, that wretched woman, hadn't managed to provoke her once. If she could hold her tongue with that nag, she could handle anything.

A small, satisfied smile tugged at her lips as she closed her eyes again, exhaustion finally pulling her under. Her body sank into the thin mattress, and this time, her sleep was deep and untroubled.

Chapter Two

At first, Rose mistook the loud pounding on her door for a fragment of her fitful dreams. She burrowed deeper into the pillows, hoping to reclaim some semblance of rest. But then a piercing female scream shattered the silence, jolting her upright in bed.

What on earth? She blinked groggily, shaking off the haze of sleep, her gaze darting around the dimly lit room

Another scream. The frantic pounding resumed.

"The beast! The beast! Someone save me from the beast!"

The terror in the voice sent Rose scrambling from the bed, her fingers fumbling for her night robe as she hurried to the door. She barely managed to wrestle the bolt free before yanking the heavy wood open.

"What in heaven's name is going on?" she snapped, rubbing at her bleary eyes as she took in the sight of a petite blonde, her wide blue eyes glistening with fear. "Why are you caterwauling like this at such an ungodly hour?"

Without waiting for an invitation, the blonde pushed her way past Rose and into the room. "Oh, please, dear lady, shut the door! Quickly!" Her voice trembled as she pressed herself against the far wall, her delicate curls trembling around her face. "He's after me!"

"He? Who's after you? Your husband?" Rose asked, though she complied, closing the door with a firm thud. She had heard rumors of husbands who mistreated their wives, brutes who used their fists rather than words, and she wondered if the poor girl before her had suffered at the hands of such a man. If so, Rose vowed silently, she would give the wretch the verbal lashing of his life. Her newly sworn ladylike demeanor could wait.

But the young woman shook her head, her golden curls bouncing wildly. "Not my husband—the beast! I had heard tales of his fearsome nature, but I never thought..." Her voice faltered, her lips trembling. "I thought I could manage, after all, he's an earl! But now... oh, I cannot bear it! I want to go home!"

Rose blinked, the young woman's words beginning to sink in. A beast? An earl? For all the blonde's eloquence, Rose had to wonder if she might be dealing with a doxy fleeing from her protector after a spat. It wouldn't be unheard of. Still, her upbringing demanded she offer aid where it was needed, no matter the circumstances.

"Did this 'beast' harm you?" Rose asked, steeling herself for an answer she feared would be dire. "Did he... attack you?"

The blonde shook her head vehemently, though her cheeks flushed a delicate shade of pink. "No, no, nothing of the sort! He's been a gentleman in that regard, but he's so... cold. So overpowering. I'm terrified of him!" Tears welled in her eyes as she clasped her hands before her. "Oh, please, you must help me escape him! I can't go back to him, I simply can't!"

Rose hesitated. The story felt... incomplete. Whoever this 'beast' was, it seemed he had yet to actually harm the girl. And yet, why else would she have fled into the night like this? But Rose had little time to ponder the full truth.

"Do you have the means to return home?" Rose asked, her tone gentle despite her doubts. Whether this woman was a courtesan or not, Rose couldn't ignore her plea for help.

"I do," the blonde sniffed, "but my bags are still in the room his lordship arranged. I daren't go back there! What if he tries to keep me captive?

Rose sighed, weighing her options. The sensible course of action would be to summon the innkeeper and let him handle the matter. But Rose suspected the man might be in league with this so-called beast—and besides, she had never been one to take the easy way out.

"You may stay here tonight," Rose decided. "In the morning, I'll send for one of the maids to collect your belongings."

"Oh, thank you! You are an angel of mercy!" The blonde clasped her hands to her chest, her blue eyes shining with gratitude. "How can I ever repay you for your kindness?"

Rose hesitated. Something about the woman's heartfelt words made her second-guess her earlier suspicions. Surely no common doxy would express such sincere gratitude. Just as she was about to ask for more details, another round of pounding rattled the door, drowning out her thoughts.

"Miss Masterson?" A deep male voice, dripping with authority, echoed through the wood. "Are you in there?"

The blonde's face turned ashen. "It's him! The beast has found me!"

"For heaven's sake, woman," the voice on the other side of the door barked, "cease this ridiculous performance and open the door at once!"

Rose's stomach dropped as she realized with horror that she had forgotten to rebolt the door. Her eyes darted around the room, searching for anything she could use as a weapon. Her gaze landed on a brass bed warmer hanging by the hearth. Without a second thought, she grabbed it, clutching it tightly as she braced herself for what was to come.

The door swung open with a creak, revealing a tall, broad-shouldered man whose dark brows were drawn together in a thunderous scowl. His emerald eyes flicked to the trembling blonde before narrowing in obvious annoyance.

"Miss Masterson," he growled, stepping further into the room, "how many times must I tell you? It is my mother who has engaged your services, not I. I am merely here to escort you to her. I have no interest in your virtue. Now, kindly return to your room and cease this tiresome charade."

"No!" The blonde shrank further against the wall, shaking her head vehemently. "I won't go with you! I won't!"

The man's eyes darkened, his jaw tightening. "Miss Masterson," he said, his voice low and dangerous, "you are testing my patience. Come with me now, or I assure you, you will regret it."

Rose had had enough of such blatant bullying. She stepped forward, raising the heavy bed warmer high above her head and then bringing it down with all he might. The blow connected solidly with the back of the intruder's head, bringing him crashing down like a felled tree.

The blonde shrieked and collapsed in a dead faint, leaving Rose standing amidst the chaos, her heart pounding in her chest.

Now what? she wondered, staring down at the two unconscious figures. Before she could even begin to formulate a plan, the room suddenly filled with strangers—guests and staff alike, all clamoring with questions and admonitions.

The commotion reached a fever pitch as the innkeeper pushed his way through the crowd, his nightcap askew as he surveyed the scene.

"Good Lord above!" he gasped, his face turning a sickly shade of white as his eyes landed on the fallen man. "You've gone and killed the bloody earl!

Chapter Three

Henry Grayson, Seventh Earl of Ashbourne, groaned as the throbbing in his head pulsed in rhythm with his heartbeat, each wave of pain more agonizing than the last. He felt as though he'd been trampled by a team of horses, and though he was not prone to self-pity, he couldn't help but wonder what in God's name had brought him to this sorry state. Oddly, he couldn't recall drinking a single glass of port, let alone enough spirits to warrant the punishment he seemed to be enduring now. Worse still, as he fought against the haze clouding his thoughts, he realized with a growing sense of alarm that he couldn't remember anything at all.

The sudden shock of that realization forced him out of the murky fog that filled his mind, his senses slowly sharpening as he struggled to focus. He was lying on the floor, that much was certain, and from the cacophony of raised voices overhead, it seemed a veritable riot was taking place around him. With great effort, he worked to separate the voices, making sense of the chaotic din.

"...in all my years!" a shrill voice rang out, unmistakably furious. "You, miss, are nothing more than a hoyden! I wonder that I was ever deceived by your simpering ways! I wouldn't stay another moment if you offered me all the gold in Prinny's vaults!"

"Considering the paltry sum that would amount to, Mrs. Nettles, I'd say you're selling your services rather cheaply," came the cutting retort, delivered in a cool, younger voice, sharp with wit. Henry would have smiled if his head wasn't splitting apart. The woman's biting reply reminded him of his mother's barbed tongue, and he made a mental note to recall the exchange—if his addled brain allowed it—for later amusement.

"We'll have to summon the constable," a whining voice interjected, laden with fear. "His lordship's a powerful man—there's no telling what he'll do once he comes to. We'll all be carted off to the colonies, I'll wager."

Henry blinked, trying to piece together the fractured puzzle of his memory. Why on earth would he wish to transport anyone? Slowly, images began to surface. He remembered arriving at an inn with his mother's new companion in tow. Miss Masterson. She had been thrilled by his attention at first, until it became evident that he had no interest in her beyond fulfilling his duty to escort her to his family estate.

From then on, she'd regarded him with skittish wariness, her nervous glances reminding him of every other woman who'd taken him for a fearsome brute. It was tiresome. He'd all but ignored her nervous energy until the maid accompanying them had knocked on his door to announce that Miss Masterson had fled. Damn and blast, he'd gone after her, more out of obligation than any true concern.

But now here he was, sprawled on the floor of some inn, with no clear recollection of how he had ended up there. His thoughts coalesced further, memories trickling in—he'd followed Miss Masterson, knocked on a door, and then...

"You hit me!" Henry groaned, his eyes flying open. Immediately, he regretted the action, as a searing white light exploded behind his eyelids. He bit back a string of curses.

"Well, of course I hit you, you miscreant" the younger woman replied, her voice filled with indignant righteousness. "You were about to attack Miss Masterson!"

The absurdity of the accusation made Henry pry his eyes open again, this time more cautiously, and he squinted at the speaker, his vision gradually sharpening. Standing before him was a woman he'd never laid eyes on in his life, though at this moment, she appeared to be his self-appointed judge and executioner.

The first thing he noticed about her was her height—tall for a woman, standing straight and proud. Then he registered the fierce spark in her caramel-colored eyes, the way her dark curls framed her face, and the undeniable beauty she exuded even while glaring daggers at him.

"Who the devil are you?" he growled, tentatively raising himself onto one elbow, fighting against the wave of dizziness that threatened to send him back to the floor.

"I am Miss Rose Sheffield," she declared, her tone defiant as her eyes flashed with a fire that matched the heat of her words. "And if you think you can transport me, you'll find yourself sorely mistaken! My great-aunt is the Dowager Countess of Waverly, and I assure you, she holds quite a bit of sway in these parts."

Henry nearly laughed at her fierce declaration, but the pain in his head checked his amusement. "Consider me properly cowed, Miss Sheffield," he replied, voice dripping with sarcasm. He raised his free hand to the side of his head, gingerly pressing against the painful lump he found there. Mercifully, he wasn't bleeding, but the knot on his skull felt large enough to warrant a full interrogation.

At least she hadn't killed him. Small mercies.

Gathering his composure, Henry's eyes narrowed as he fixed her with an icy stare. "Tell me, Miss Sheffield, do you make a habit of bludgeoning innocent men when they knock on your door? Or is this some special treatment reserved solely for me?"

"Are you all right, my lord?" The innkeeper, a short, plump man with anxious eyes, shouldered his way past Miss Sheffield, his hands wringing nervously as he stared down at Henry. "I've sent for Dr. Martin, and I can have the constable here in a trice, if you'd like."

Henry's gaze flicked back to Miss Sheffield. Despite her defiant stance and sharp words, he saw the flicker of unease in her proud expression. Her teeth worried at her bottom lip, betraying her nerves. For a brief, absurd moment, he admired the lush ripeness of those lips before shaking the thought away, forcing his attention back to the matter at hand.

"The constable may enjoy his sleep," Henry said, pushing himself into a sitting position with a wince. "I see no need to disturb him... yet." He scanned the room, trying to piece together the chaos. "Where is Miss Masterson?"

"If you are referring to that poor girl you were attempting to assault," Miss Sheffield interjected sharply, her smile edged with smug satisfaction, "she is not here. And you ought to be ashamed of yourself for forcing your attentions on such a gently bred young lady."

Henry's hand clenched at his side, his temper flaring like a whip of fire. "That is the second time you've accused me of dishonoring my name and my title," he said, his voice low, laced with danger. "I would not recommend you try for a third."

He noted the flicker of apprehension in her eyes, but to her credit, Miss Sheffield remained silent. Henry glared at her, taking in the tousled curls framing her face, and only now did he notice that she was dressed in a night robe. In fact, everyone in the room, including the fretful innkeeper, appeared to have been roused from their beds. His dark brows drew together as the full implications of the situation sank in.

"You've dragged me into a lady's bedchamber," he growled, his gaze narrowing at Miss Sheffield, "and you dare to accuse me? What kind of scheme are you running here? Why did Miss Masterson flee to you? If I find that you're in league with her—"

If he expected to intimidate or cow Miss Sheffield, he was sorely mistaken. Rather than shrinking back in fear or sputtering in indignation, she stood tall, her head held high, tossing back her curls with a regal defiance that startled him. Her eyes burned with fury, her voice sharp as a dagger's edge.

"If you truly believe I lured you into my bedchamber, then you are even more of a doltish beast than I first suspected!" She snapped, ignoring the collective gasps from the onlookers. "Now, kindly remove yourself from my room. You may await the doctor elsewhere."

Henry's lips thinned as his temper flared anew. It had been years since anyone had spoken to him with such blatant disrespect, and every instinct in him screamed to retaliate. But the situation was delicate. Any further outburst on his part could cause a scandal he could ill afford. For now, he knew he had no choice but to retreat, a thought that rankled deeply.

"As you say, Miss Sheffield," he replied tightly, motioning for the innkeeper to help him to his feet. The shorter man scrambled forward, awkwardly bracing Henry's weight as they struggled to haul him upright. With a few grunts and more effort than Henry cared to admit, he was finally standing, though the room tilted dangerously as he fought off another wave of dizziness.

Drawing himself up to his full height, Henry glared down at Miss Sheffield. His voice, when he spoke, was cold and cutting. "Do not think this is the end of the matter, madam. We will be having a conversation first thing tomorrow morning. And if you have any thoughts of sneaking away, I would strongly advise against it. Your great-aunt may be the Dowager Countess of Waverly, but I am the Earl of Ashbourne. You will find my influence in this village to be... substantial. Do you understand?"

Miss Sheffield's cheeks flushed a deep shade of crimson, her temper clearly simmering just beneath the surface. But her tone remained clipped, civil. "Yes, my lord," she bit out.

"Good," Henry said, giving her a curt nod before allowing the innkeeper to assist him out of the room, his ears filled with the man's incessant stream of apologies. He didn't bother to respond. His mind was too preoccupied with the simmering rage coursing through his veins and the vow forming in his thoughts.

He would make Miss Sheffield regret crossing him. If it was the last thing he did.

"Well, I hope you are satisfied!" Mrs. Nettles wasted no time voicing her displeasure the moment the door closed behind the Earl. "Disgrace and ruin—that's what you've brought down on all our heads! You mark my words, we'll be taken up for this, and if you think I mean to suffer for your folly, you are sorely mistaken! I shall tell his lordship I had no part in this..." she gestured wildly, "...this display!" Her eyes narrowed, her lips curling in a sneer. "And when I return home, you can be sure I'll inform the vicar of your conduct. Not that it will surprise him in the least. He warned me about you. He said you were nothing but a limb of Satan. Would that I had listened!"

"And would that I had listened to my solicitor," Rose shot back, rubbing her temples. "He told me you were a shrew of the first order, and it seems he was right." The sharp retort came out more forcefully than Rose had intended, her patience worn thin after the night's chaos. The thrill of defiance faded quickly, leaving behind only a hollow weariness. All she craved now was a moment's peace, but it appeared even that modest desire would be hard won.

Mrs. Nettles' mouth flapped open and closed, resembling a fish gasping for breath. "Well, of all the ungrateful, ill-mannered women it has been my misfortune to encounter!" she sputtered, her voice rising an octave. "You, Miss Sheffield, are nothing but a hussy, and I'll have no more of it. Our association is at an end! Good night!" With that, she spun on her heel, her hooked nose held high as she stormed out of the room, slamming the door behind her.

"And good riddance to you, you old cat!" Maggie muttered as she snapped the door closed again with a satisfying thud. She turned back to Rose, her face lighting up with grim satisfaction. "If I'd known that smashing a bed warmer over a lord's head was all it took to be rid of that biddy, I'd have done it myself days ago!

Rose allowed herself a small, tired smile at Maggie's words. "Perhaps that's what Dryden meant about everything being good for something," she said, but the humor quickly ebbed as the reality of the situation settled in. "But Maggie..." Her brow furrowed, concern clouding her features. "Do you think his lordship will have me arrested?"

The maid's expression sobered, her earlier amusement fading. "As to that, Miss, there's no telling," she said, nervously wringing her hands. "He did seem rather put out with you, but maybe he'll be in better spirits once his head's stopped aching. Besides, it's him who barged into your bedchamber. No judge worth his salt would fault you for protecting yourself however you could."

Rose nodded slowly, Maggie's reasoning easing some of her anxiety. "There's truth in that," she agreed, a flicker of confidence returning as she imagined how she might present her case should the Earl indeed drag her before a magistrate. She could already picture herself in her primmest gown, her head held high, casting herself as the very picture of a well-bred lady thrust into a compromising situation through no fault of her own. Naturally, she would express her deep regret over the misunderstanding, tearfully explaining how she'd had no choice but to defend her honor.

She was even toying with the idea of invoking her father's memory, her eyes growing misty at the thought of playing the orphan card, when a sharp pang of guilt jolted her back to reality.

Good Lord, I'm doing it again, she thought with a shudder. Plotting, scheming—twisting things so I can have my own way. And to stoop so low as to use her father's death in such a way... The thought made her stomach churn.

"Miss Rose?" Maggie's voice broke through her spiraling thoughts, her face pinched with concern. "Are you all right? You've gone white as a sheet!"

Rose managed a weak smile. "I'm fine," she lied. "Just tired. I think I'd best try to get some rest. I have a feeling I'll need it."

"Aye, that's true enough," Maggie said, bustling over to help Rose into bed. "Though how you'll sleep after all this ruckus, I don't know. That reminds me, where's that young woman who started all this? Miss Masterson, was it? I've not seen so much as a glimpse of her since you walloped his lordship."

Rose frowned, suddenly realizing that she hadn't given Miss Masterson much thought since the Earl had stormed in. Somehow, amidst the chaos, the girl had managed to slip away unnoticed. "I don't know where she is," Rose admitted, her unease growing.

Maggie shrugged, apparently unbothered. "Well, I reckon she'll turn up by breakfast," she said dismissively. "Now, you just close your eyes and try to rest. You'll want to look your best when you face his lordship again."

Rose chuckled softly at Maggie's fussing, feeling her body sag with exhaustion as she sank deeper into the mattress. "You haven't called me sweeting in years," she murmured, her eyes drifting closed.

"Haven't I?" Maggie tugged the blankets up to Rose's chin, her touch surprisingly gentle for all her gruffness.

"Maybe it's because I haven't been very sweet," Rose mumbled, the words barely a whisper as she surrendered to the pull of sleep.

"Good night, Maggie," she managed before the heaviness of her eyelids won the battle, and she slipped into a peaceful slumber.

"Good night, Miss Rose," Maggie whispered, brushing a stray curl from her mistress's forehead before retreating into the shadows, leaving the room quiet once more.

Chapter Four

"What do you mean she isn't here?" Henry Grayson, the Earl of Ashbourne, bellowed, wincing as the sharp pain in his head throbbed in rhythm with his rising fury. He swore under his breath, tempering his voice before speaking again. "How the devil did she manage to get away?" He turned a hard, accusatory gaze on the maid, Mabel, who seemed entirely too calm for his liking. "I thought I brought you along to keep an eye on her."

"And so you did, my lord," Mabel replied, unaffected by his irritation, her tone cool as a winter's breeze. "But even maids must rest, and the little minx slipped away while I was sleeping. Took her bags with her too, so I reckon there's no point in looking. She's likely halfway to Bedford by now."

Henry clenched his jaw at her words, guilt pricking at his temper. "I didn't mean to suggest you were negligent," he muttered, rubbing his temples. The pounding in his skull was relentless, more likely from the vile concoction that blasted doctor had forced down his throat than the actual blow from the bed warmer. He hadn't felt this wretched since his days at Oxford, and he swore he'd rather endure another year of lambing than another moment of this torment.

"This is all my mother's doing," he grumbled, lowering his hand as he met Mabel's gaze, frustration simmering beneath his tone. "Why couldn't she have just sent for this companion like she has with all the others? Why must I be the one to fetch her?"

Mabel's eyes gleamed knowingly, though Henry, too focused on his misery, missed the look. "Miss Masterson is the great-niece of a viscount, my lord," Mabel said, her lips pursing in a tight line. "You can't expect a lady of her standing to take the mail coach like a commoner."

"I don't see why not," Henry retorted, still irritable and decidedly unwilling to absolve his mother of blame. He'd been in the thick of lambing season when she'd insisted he journey south to meet her newly hired companion. He'd refused at first, citing more important duties, but the loneliness in his mother's eyes had eventually worn him down. Now, it seemed, his efforts had all been in vain.

He sighed heavily. "I suppose I'll have to return to Bedford and hire another woman for Mother," he grumbled, feeling increasingly put out at the thought. "Unless..." he paused, a glimmer of hope lightening his dark mood. "Do you think we might find someone suitable here?"

Mabel raised a brow, clearly unimpressed with the prospect. "I reckon we could ask around, my lord, but her ladyship has particular notions, and you know how she is. You can't just hire any woman. Though..."

Henry scowled at the hesitation in her voice. "Though what?"

"That young lady, Miss Sheffield..." Mabel's tone turned thoughtful. "She's quite something, don't you think?"

Henry's expression darkened at the mention of the woman who had laid him flat with a bed warmer. "How am I to know?" he snapped, though the memory of her honey-brown eyes and riot of dark curls rose unbidden in his mind. "The woman bashed me over the head before I had the chance to say so much as hello!"

Mabel offered a nonchalant shrug, seemingly undeterred. "Shows she's quick-witted. The countess would like that. She doesn't care for empty-headed females."

"Then she would have been sorely disappointed with Miss Masterson," Henry observed dryly, bitterness creeping into his voice. "The chit was a featherbrain."

Mabel sighed wistfully, as if mourning the loss of beauty rather than brains. "But so pretty, though. Like a little porcelain doll, she was."

Henry said nothing, though Mabel's words confirmed what he had long suspected. His mother's main requirement for her companions wasn't competence or intellect but rather physical beauty, hoping, no doubt, that one of them would catch his eye and sway his heart. He sneered at the thought. After his dismal Season in London, he had no illusions about women of his class—or their lack of interest in a man like him, title and wealth notwithstanding.

"My lord?" Mabel's sharp tone broke through his bitter musings, bringing him back to the present.

Henry blinked, realizing she'd been trying to get his attention. "Apologies, Mabel. What were you saying?"

"I said you might at least speak with Miss Sheffield," she repeated, her bluntness reflective of her years in service to the family. "Perhaps she would consider taking the position."

Henry raised a brow. "The niece of the Dowager Countess of Waverly?" he asked, recalling Miss Sheffield's haughty claim. "I shouldn't think that likely. Besides, I'd rather not give her another chance to finish the job she started on my skull last night." He rubbed the sore lump on his head, wincing at the reminder.

"Provided she is the countess's niece," Mabel added, ignoring his protest.

Henry's eyes narrowed. "You don't think she is?"

Mabel shrugged. "The innkeeper mentioned the countess has a townhouse in the village. If Miss Sheffield was truly related to her, you'd think she'd be staying there, not at an inn."

Henry mulled over her words. Mabel was right—a countess wouldn't allow her niece to lodge in a public inn. Still, something about Miss Sheffield's regal bearing had convinced him she was telling the truth. There had been a quiet authority in the way she'd carried herself, a confidence that was hard to fake.

Perhaps it was more than her carriage, he mused, recalling her defiant gaze and the fierce determination in her voice. She had been a hellcat, yes, but one with a fire in her that intrigued him. She'd looked ready to face down the devil himself if need be, and he found himself grudgingly admiring her spirit.

"I suppose I could speak with her," he conceded, coming to a decision. "What harm could it do?"

Rose spent most of the morning preparing herself for the inevitable confrontation with the Earl. After much consideration, she settled on appearing coolly penitent, remorseful even, but certainly not fearful. An apology was in order, of course, but she would offer it as a lady ought to—gracefully, with no hint of submission. After all, as Maggie had wisely pointed out, it was he who had barged into her room. The scandal of the situation was far more his to explain than hers.

Mrs. Nettles had, predictably, made good on her threat and departed in high dudgeon on the southbound mail coach, taking Miss Masterson with her. Rose wished them both the joy of each other's company and felt a weight lift from her shoulders at their absence.

When the inn's saucy maid arrived to inform her that "His lordship" awaited her in the private parlor, Rose hid her trepidation behind a carefully composed expression. She had chosen a gown of dove-gray merino, trimmed with lavender and black ribbons at the hem and throat—a modest dress, yet one that showed her to great advantage. If the Earl took pity on her because she was in mourning, well, she assured herself with a final glance in the mirror, that would hardly be her fault.

The first thing she noticed upon entering the cramped parlor was the extravagant fire roaring in the sooty grate. Last night, when she had bespoken the same room, it had taken a bribe just to coax an indifferent fire from wet coal. Evidently, the innkeeper thought only earls were worthy of seasoned wood, she mused with a sniff of disapproval.

"Close the door, Miss Sheffield, unless you wish the entire town to eavesdrop on our conversation," came the cold, clipped voice from her right.

She turned just as the Earl rose to his feet, and whatever apology she'd prepared froze on her lips. Good heavens. The man was a veritable giant.

Dressed in an unfashionable blue velvet coat that strained to contain his broad shoulders, his jet-black hair caught back in a queue no one had worn in decades, the Earl was quite unlike any man she had ever encountered. His height, she remembered from last night, but in the frenzy of the moment, she had somehow overlooked the sheer size of him. The realization sent a bolt of uncertainty through her. For a fleeting moment, she considered fleeing just as Miss Masterson had—but no. She was a lady, not a mouse. She would not bolt.

"I trust you will not find it too unseemly if I leave the door slightly ajar, your lordship," she said, her voice cool and steady. "Without a chaperone, propriety must be observed."

He raised a brow, amusement flickering in his dark green eyes. "Are you afraid I might harm you, Miss Sheffield?" His tone was mocking. "I should remind you it was you who assaulted me, and without any provocation, I might add."

Rose flushed at the taunt, her earlier decision to behave with grace swiftly forgotten. "Some might consider a man forcing his way into a lady's bedchamber to be sufficient provocation for more than just a bed warmer to the head." She tossed her head defiantly. "And you certainly don't look like any earl I've ever seen."

The Earl's easy smile faded, replaced by a glint of cold steel in his eyes. "So I've been told. But make no mistake, I am an Earl, and it is a crime to assault a member of the House of Lords. Would you care to know the punishment for such an offense?"

Rose straightened, forcing herself not to flinch beneath the weight of his glare. "I am aware of the consequences, my lord."

"It's transportation to a penal colony," he continued, ignoring her. "And don't think your sex will shield you. The magistrate here has little sympathy for criminals, male or female."

"I am not a criminal!"

"Nor am I," he returned smoothly, his gaze hardening. "And I do not take kindly to being treated as one merely because I do not fit your expectations of what an Earl should be. Now, shut the door, and sit. You have my word I won't harm you."

Rose sighed, biting back a retort as she closed the door with a sharp click. "I was merely observing proprieties," she muttered under her breath as she crossed the room and took the chair he indicated.

"Do you always do what is proper, Miss Sheffield?" His eyes held a hint of amusement, though his tone was unreadable.

"I have been trying," she replied, folding her hands primly in her lap. "Though it seems my efforts are wasted. I've yet to see any benefit from my restraint."

"Indeed?" The single word was drawn out, making Rose look up sharply. A half-smile softened his harsh features, and she was disarmed for a moment by how much less fearsome he appeared when he wasn't glaring down at her.

Focus, she reminded herself. "What is it you wished to discuss?"

"A great deal, actually." He settled back in his chair, his posture casual, though Rose sensed the intensity simmering beneath the surface. "However, if it puts your mind at ease, my mother's maid will be joining us shortly. She's fetching tea."

"Your mother is here?" Rose asked, genuinely surprised.

"Sadly, no." His deep voice took on a rueful note. "Had she been, I wouldn't find myself in this predicament. My mother is... formidable. She wouldn't have let Miss Masterson slip through her fingers. You would like her, I think."

"I'm sure I would," Rose murmured, though she wasn't entirely certain where this conversation was headed.

Before she could ask, the door opened, and a plump maid entered, balancing a tray laden with tea and cakes.

"I've seen better food in a pig's trough," the maid grumbled as she set the tray down in front of Rose. "Stale bread, cakes as hard as rocks. Had to threaten the cook before she'd do a proper tea."

"Thank you, Mabel." The Earl took her complaints in stride, barely sparing the maid a glance. "Now, sit down and be quiet. I'm not done speaking with Miss Sheffield."

"You can talk while you eat." Mabel ignored him, loading a plate and handing it to Rose. "Your maid said you barely touched your breakfast."

Rose stifled a smile, charmed by the maid's brusque manner. "Thank you, Mabel. You're very kind."

Several moments passed as Mabel fussed with the tea and sandwiches. The Earl looked decidedly uncomfortable, his large hands awkwardly trying to balance the delicate cup and saucer. Rose felt a small thrill of satisfaction as she watched him. He looked like a bear in a bonnet, and she found herself hoping he'd crush the fragile porcelain just to see what would happen.

"You mentioned last night that you are related to the Countess of Waverly." His words, delivered without preamble, startled her from her musings. He was watching her closely, his eyes narrowed.

"Yes," Rose replied, bristling at the skepticism lacing his tone. "She is my great-aunt."

"And yet, here you are, staying in an inn." He took a sip of tea, his gaze never leaving hers. "One would think a countess would provide more suitable accommodations for a relative, unmarried or not."

The insinuation in his voice made her hands tighten around her cup. She longed to throw the contents in his smug face but resisted. "Apparently, her ladyship did not receive my letter. She's in Scotland visiting her son. The staff, not knowing me, could not allow me to stay."

"And what of your family in... Richmond, was it?"

Rose blinked in surprise. I never told him where I'm from. "Yes. Richmond."

"Would your family not prefer you return to them, rather than linger here?"

Her throat tightened. "I have no family, my lord. My father passed last year. My mother when I was a child." She forced herself to meet his gaze, waiting for his reaction

A flicker of sympathy softened his features. "I see. I should have known by your dress." His voice gentled. "My condolences, Miss Sheffield. I understand what it is to lose a parent."

His unexpected kindness made Rose's stomach twist with guilt. *This is far easier when he's being insufferable,* she thought, struggling to maintain her composure.

"Why are you asking about my family?" she asked quietly, setting her cup down before her trembling hands could betray her.

"It's of no importance," he replied, though the hard look in his eyes told her otherwise. "However, knowing that you are somewhat... unattached makes things simpler."

"Things?" A chill ran down her spine.

"Such as your returning to Derbyshire with me to act as my mother's companion." His tone was maddeningly calm, his smile cool and self-assured. "You deprived me of one companion, Miss Sheffield. It seems only fair you replace her."

Chapter Five

Henry almost chuckled at the incredulous look on Miss Sheffield's face. She resembled a child caught with a hand hovering over a plate of sweets, just as the nanny raised a ruler to rap her knuckles.

"I beg your pardon, my lord?" Her brow furrowed in obvious confusion.

"I wish you to act as my mother's companion," he repeated, leaning back in his chair, relishing the moment. It was time to close the trap he'd been laying since she walked in. "She is an invalid, unable to travel. Miss Masterson was to take up that role, but thanks to your... interference, my mother is now without a companion."

Rose's teacup clattered onto the saucer, her temper flaring. "Oh, for pity's sake! You make it sound as though the poor girl was your prisoner! For your information, sir, I did not interfere. Miss Masterson came to me. I didn't seek her out!"

"Perhaps not." Henry shrugged. "But there's no denying that, had you not... assisted her, I would still have a companion for my mother.

I love my mother, Miss Sheffield, and I detest the thought that I might have failed her."

Her face paled at his words, the flush of anger draining away. "What do you mean by that?" she asked, her voice trembling.

His frown deepened. He hadn't meant to frighten her. His imposing figure had always been a weapon he used with care, never wanting to intimidate unless absolutely necessary. That he'd done so now, even unintentionally, unsettled him. He softened his tone.

"I mean," he said gently, "that after traveling from Derbyshire to Bedford to fetch Miss Masterson, I have no intention of returning home empty-handed. I propose that you and your maid accompany me. You can serve as my mother's companion until we find a replacement."

Rose remained silent, her hands twisting in her lap. Henry cursed himself inwardly. Perhaps Mabel had been wrong to suggest this course. He should have apologized first, not barged in like a madman the night before. No wonder she'd hit him with a bed warmer. He sent her a tentative look, then cautiously reached out to touch her hand.

"Are you all right?" he asked, his tone softer now. "I'm sorry if I upset you. That wasn't my intention."

Rose looked up at him, unsure of what to say. In the end, only the truth would suffice. She took a steadying breath. "I'm not upset, my lord. It's just..." She hesitated, meeting his piercing green gaze. "I know what it is to disappoint someone. I can understand your predicament."

Henry frowned, guilt settling heavily in his chest. Perhaps he was a beast, as people so often whispered behind his back. He'd certainly been nothing short of beastly since encountering Rose Sheffield.

"My father died last year," Rose continued quietly. "We quarreled incessantly before his death. I know what it feels like to be a disappointment. I don't blame him for disinheriting me."

His brows shot up. "Disinherited you?" He could hardly believe any father would treat his own daughter so cruelly.

Rose's cheeks flushed. She hadn't meant to blurt that out. "It's not as grim as it sounds," she said with a forced laugh. "My mother left me well-provided for. I'm far from destitute."

Henry remained silent, unconvinced. He opened his mouth to offer her the position as a permanent solution, but she spoke first.

"I've been thinking," Rose said, her voice stronger now. "I'll come with you to Derbyshire and act as your mother's temporary companion. It seems only fair."

Henry narrowed his eyes. "So you admit fault?"

"Not at all." Her chin lifted, her defiance returning. "This entire mess is your doing from start to finish. But I see no reason why your mother should suffer for your mistakes."

"My mistakes?" His guilt vanished, replaced by incredulity.

Rose nodded briskly. "If you hadn't frightened Miss Masterson, she wouldn't have fled to my room for sanctuary. And I certainly wouldn't have had to knock you over the head with a bed warmer." She paused, then added, "Though I suppose you didn't mean to frighten her. She struck me as having a rather excitable nature."

Henry stared at her in disbelief. "You don't think I meant to ravish her?"

Rose's eyes turned icy. "Had I thought that, my lord, I'd have told you to go straight to the devil. Now, if you're quite finished trying to make me blush, when would you like to depart?"

"I hope you know what you're about," Maggie grumbled as she carefully folded a chemise and placed it in the trunk at her feet. "Your father would have a thing or two to say if he knew what you were up to."

Rose smiled faintly, the memory of one of her last quarrels with her father flickering in her mind. "Nonsense, Maggie. Papa wouldn't be the slightest bit surprised by my actions," she said with a light laugh that masked the ache in her chest. "Didn't I once threaten to run away and become a governess if he didn't listen to me?"

Maggie snorted in that eloquent way of hers, making her opinion on the matter clear. "Governesses is one thing; companions is another," she said, adding another chemise to the pile. "At least that Mabel seems a sensible soul. She'll keep his lordship in line, no doubt about it."

The image of the towering earl being bossed about by his mother's maid made Rose smile despite her heavy heart. "She does seem to have him under her thumb, doesn't she? I wonder how she manages it."

"Never you mind how she does it," Maggie replied with a huff. "You should be more concerned about how your great-aunt's going to react when she finds out you've gone dashing off to Derbyshire with the Earl. That'll take some explaining, mark my words."

Rose had already thought about that particular dilemma. "Don't worry, Maggie. Aunt will be positively delighted to learn that the Countess of Ashbourne, upon hearing of my tragic situation, invited me to stay with her in her lovely country home. How could she possibly object to that?"

Maggie's eyes narrowed as she slammed the trunk lid shut. "She'll object plenty when she finds out the Countess wasn't even in London! And if you think no one's going to tell her the truth, you've gone daft. There'll be more than enough busybodies eager to spill the tale."

"Perhaps," Rose said with a calm smile. "But Aunt will accept my version of events."

Maggie frowned, clearly unconvinced. "Why?"

Rose's lips curved into a knowing smile. "Because it's convenient for her to believe it. If I've learned anything, it's that people always believe what's easiest for them. The truth has very little to do with reality."

Maggie stared at her, shaking her head in disbelief. "I still don't see why you're so set on going to Derbyshire," she grumbled. "I'd have thought after last night, you'd never want to clap eyes on his lordship again."

Rose hesitated, unsure of how to explain. She lowered her gaze to her lap, fingers absently tracing the lace on her gown as she searched for the right words. "Maybe," she said softly, "maybe it's a way to make amends with Papa. I failed him so terribly, Maggie. And I see no reason why the Earl should fail his mother because of me." She shrugged, trying to appear nonchalant. "Besides, it's only for a little while, and Derbyshire is bound to be more agreeable than Richmond." She added a light chuckle, but Maggie's scowl made it clear her attempt at humor had fallen flat.

"Failed your father, indeed," Maggie muttered darkly, rolling up a stocking and tossing it into the second trunk. "If you ask me, he failed you! Cutting you out of his will just because you didn't want to marry that mutton-headed cousin of yours... Well—" She shook her head fiercely. "Far be it from me to speak ill of the dead, but I hope he's properly sorry for what he did."

"That was just money," Rose countered softly, trying once again to make Maggie understand. "I failed him in far deeper ways, and I'm determined to make amends, however I can." She stood, her shoulders squared as if bracing herself for the weight of her decision. "Now, please finish the packing. His lordship wishes to leave as soon as possible."

They set out after a hasty luncheon, heading north in the Earl's grand traveling coach. The carriage amused Rose—it was as large and imposing as Ashbourne himself. Painted a sleek, gleaming black with only gold and scarlet trim for decoration, the vehicle was completely free of the usual heraldic crests. She found it odd that a man so clearly aware of his rank as the Earl of Ashbourne would choose to travel in something so devoid of adornment. It seemed uncharacteristic, or perhaps she didn't know him as well as she thought.

Maggie and Mabel had become fast friends, immediately settling into comfortable gossip, while Rose sat back and stared out the glazed window at the passing countryside. She would have preferred to spend the journey becoming better acquainted with the Earl, but after a curt, "Good day," he'd buried his nose in a gazette. His indifference stung her pride more than she cared to admit. After all, she reminded herself, she was doing the man a considerable favor. The least he could do was acknowledge her existence!

She turned her gaze from the window to him. His head was bent, his attention fixed entirely on whatever he was reading. If he refused to satisfy her understandable curiosity, then she would simply discern what she could on her own, she thought with a flash of mischief.

He was dressed for travel in a gray wool coat, the many capes making him appear even more imposing than usual. Upon entering the coach, he had tossed his hat and gloves aside with a careless gesture, suggesting he rarely bothered with such items. His large, work-worn hands confirmed that observation. His dark hair, pulled back as it had been that morning, struck her as old-fashioned—more a style suited to men of her father's generation—but it oddly suited Ashbourne. A smile tugged at her lips as she imagined him in the latest fashion, with Byron-esque curls framing his face.

"Is there something I can do for you, Miss Sheffield?" The Earl's cold voice dissolved the amusing vision, and Rose blinked to find his piercing green eyes watching her.

She flushed, caught gaping at him like a schoolgirl. "I was wondering about your mother, my lord," she said, masking her embarrassment with a light tone. "I believe you mentioned she is an invalid?"

His expression grew more remote as he turned to look out the window. "She was injured in a fall last year and has not walked since." His clipped tone made it clear the subject was a painful one. "The doctors have no explanation for it, but then, they rarely do."

The grief in his voice made Rose forget her annoyance. "I'm terribly sorry, my lord," she murmured, meaning it.

"It was my fault," he continued, his hands clenching into fists. "We had guests—some fools wanting to hunt. I've never seen the sense in chasing defenseless animals, so I refused to join them. I thought that would be the end of it, but my mother's sense of duty won out. She took them out herself, and she lost her seat going over a hedge."

Rose gasped. One of her neighbors' sons had died in a similar accident, and the boy had been in the prime of life. The Countess must have been in her fifties—how she'd survived at all was a miracle. Rose wanted to say something comforting, but the bleak look on the Earl's face told her words would offer him little solace.

"That is why I am so determined you should act as her companion until I can find a replacement," he said, his gaze locking on her face once more. "I put her in that damn chair. The least I can do is make sure she has everything she needs."

Rose's heart sank at his declaration. She had wanted to understand the Earl better, and it seemed she had gotten her wish. Unsure of how to respond, she turned back to the window.

Henry watched her in silence, cursing himself for revealing so much. He was a taciturn man by nature, and yet he'd poured his heart out to her. It was her eyes, he realized with a frown. Those direct, clear eyes of hers seemed to see straight through to his soul. Her dark-brown hair was elegantly pulled back, but he could still remember how it had looked when it tumbled down her back, tousled from sleep. She was dressed impeccably in a traveling gown of gray and maroon, a sight as lovely and delicate as Dresden china. How could this woman be the same hellcat who had knocked him over the head with a bed warmer?

The silence between them stretched, thick and uncomfortable, as the coach continued its journey northward. Even Mabel and Maggie had quieted, and by the time they arrived at the inn where they were to take tea, Rose's nerves were frayed. Her head ached from the tension and the constant swaying of the coach, and when she stepped down from the carriage, her knees nearly buckled. She would have stumbled if not for the Earl's steady hand at her elbow.

"Are you all right, Miss Sheffield?" His tone was uncharacteristically solicitous as he studied her pale features. "Shall I carry you?"

The thought of being carried into the inn like some swooning schoolgirl was all it took to stiffen Rose's spine. "I'm perfectly fine, my lord," she said firmly, staring past his broad shoulder. "My foot slipped on a rock, that's all."

He gave her a measured look but took a step back, allowing her to continue on her own. They were greeted by the innkeeper, who ushered them into a private parlor with a fire roaring in the hearth. After washing her hands and face, Rose hurried to the warmth of the fire. She was on her second cup of tea when the Earl joined her.

"We should reach Derbyshire by evening," he said, his eyes intent on her face. "Are you certain you're up for continuing? You're still quite pale."

His concern pleased Rose, though it also irritated her. She despised women who wilted at the slightest hardship, and it annoyed her that he should take her for one of them. Yet, at the same time, she couldn't recall the last time anyone had shown such interest in her well-being. It was oddly touching—and because she liked it too much, she pushed the feeling away with a scowl.

"I assumed after last night, you'd know I'm not one to wilt at the slightest breeze," she said, lifting her chin and meeting his piercing green eyes. "A carriage ride is well within my capabilities, I assure you."

Her belligerent tone and defiant posture seemed to have no effect on him. "We'll leave within the hour," he said smoothly, his voice as cold as ice. Then, without another word, he stood and left the room.

Rose watched him go, feeling more than a little ashamed of her shrewish display. So much for her vow to conduct herself as a lady, she thought with an unhappy sigh. It seemed this newfound resolve would be far more challenging to maintain than she had anticipated.

Chapter Six

It was twilight by the time they arrived at Ashbourne Hall, nestled just three miles outside Derby. The sprawling estate came into view as the coach passed through wrought-iron gates, and Rose felt her breath catch at the sight of the grand house, its façade bathed in the fading light. The manor had been built in the previous century, its symmetrical lines and soaring columns lending it an air of timeless elegance.

"It's beautiful," Rose whispered, her voice tinged with awe as she turned to Henry.

He looked out at the familiar sight, the quiet pride of ownership evident in his voice. "Yes, it is," he said simply, before gesturing towards the entrance. "Shall we? I expect my mother will want to meet you."

Rose felt a twinge of nerves but nodded. However, upon their arrival inside, Mabel hurried to inform them that the countess had already retired for the evening. With a brief apology, she disappeared upstairs to attend her mistress, and Maggie followed suit to tend to the unpacking.

This left Rose and Henry awkwardly standing in the entryway, neither quite sure what to do. Finally, Henry broke the silence.

"We keep to country hours here," he said, clearing his throat and making an obvious attempt at politeness. "Dinner will be served shortly. You're welcome to join me in an hour if you wish."

Rose hesitated, aware that he was extending an olive branch. Still, the idea of a hot bath and the comfort of a soft bed after the long journey held more appeal than attempting small talk over dinner. She offered a small, apologetic smile.

"If it's all the same to you, my lord, I think I'll have a tray sent up. It's been a rather long day."

His expression was unreadable as he nodded. "As you wish. I'll bid you goodnight then." He paused, as though considering something, before adding, "I'll be gone early tomorrow, but after luncheon, I'd be happy to show you around the estate. Do you ride?"

Rose debated how much to reveal, then sighed. There was no use pretending expertise where none existed. "After a fashion," she admitted with a small laugh. "We only rented horses on occasion, and I rode when visiting friends in the country. But I'm a quick study, my lord," she added, her voice hopeful.

A smile tugged at the corners of his mouth, and the warmth in his green eyes startled her. "Of that, Miss Sheffield, I have no doubt," he drawled, before inclining his head. "Until tomorrow then."

The room Rose was shown to was more luxurious than anything she had ever experienced. Its bright yellow walls were adorned with delicate Oriental prints, and the furniture was a charming mix of Queen Anne elegance and rococo grandeur. After indulging in a long soak in the copper tub, Rose slipped into the high, canopied bed, savoring the feel of the soft linens as she picked at the tea and cakes brought to her by a giggling maid.

"It seems I've been misled about the plight of companions all these years," she remarked dryly to Maggie, who was arranging her belongings on the polished dressing table. "It's hardly as grim as I imagined. Quite comfortable, in fact."

Maggie, ever the realist, gave her a skeptical look. "Don't let the finery fool you, Miss Sheffield. This is a guest room, not the sort of quarters you'd get if you were a proper companion. Though I'll grant you," she added grudgingly, "even the servants' rooms here aren't so bad. I've got my own room, would you believe."

"You do?" Rose was genuinely impressed. At home, Maggie had always shared her room with the other maid in a cramped space beneath the eaves. "The house must be enormous."

"Thirty rooms, not counting the servants' quarters," Maggie said, repeating what Mabel had told her. "There's a town house in London too, though it hasn't been used in years."

Rose's eyelids grew heavy as the warmth of the fire, the bath, and the comfort of the bed took their toll. "Really?" she asked around a yawn. "Why not?"

"Mabel didn't say," Maggie replied, folding the last of Rose's garments. "But it's something to do with the earl. Apparently, his lordship refuses to go to London. Not even for Parliament."

"Mmm," Rose murmured, already half-asleep. Her last fleeting thought before sleep overtook her was a vague curiosity about why someone as duty-bound as the Earl of Ashbourne would shirk such an important responsibility. It was something she'd have to ask him about—eventually.

"So, you're the young lady who tried to kill my son with a bed warmer." Lady Beatrice Grayson's bright-green eyes, identical to her son's, sparkled with amusement as she greeted Rose. "Well, I suppose

I should be grateful your aim wasn't any better. Come closer, let me have a proper look at you."

Rose bit back a smile as she obeyed the countess's teasing command. She had expected to find an ailing, fragile woman in the countess's bedchamber, but Lady Beatrice, draped in an elegant gown of lilac silk, was anything but an invalid. Indeed, if she weren't sitting in a chair, Rose might have thought the earl had been spinning her a tale.

"Ah, that's better." Lady Beatrice's lips curved in a pleased smile as she studied Rose with unabashed curiosity. "Yes, you'll do nicely, I think. What did you say your name was?"

"I am Miss Rose Sheffield, my lady," Rose replied, noting how the earl's strong features—his full mouth and high cheekbones—were mirrored in his mother's face. "My great-aunt is Lady Waverly. Do you know her?"

"Charlotte? Oh, I certainly do. But don't worry, I shan't hold that against you," the countess replied with a tinkling laugh. "None of us are to blame for our relations, thank heavens. My own family, I fear, leaves much to be desired. Wigs, you know."

"No, my lady, I didn't," Rose answered, thinking what a pity it was that the earl hadn't inherited his mother's warmth and wit along with her striking looks. "But I shall be sure not to speak ill of them."

"Oh, feel free! You couldn't possibly say anything worse than what Henry says. A Tory, like his father, though he pays as much attention to politics as he does to fashion. Sheep, on the other hand—now, there's a topic he adores. Do you know anything about sheep?"

The unexpected turn in conversation made Rose laugh. "No, my lady, I can't say that I do," she said, thinking that she might very well enjoy the coming days in Lady Beatrice's company. Perhaps there was no need to rush the earl in finding a new companion.

The countess sighed dramatically. "What a shame. I had hoped for an ally. But never mind. Shall we have tea, then? I'll tell you all about our home, and you can tell me about yourself. I'm dying to hear more about the young woman who bested my son."

Rose's first morning at Thornfield Manor passed pleasantly, with Lady Beatrice proving to be a charming companion. By luncheon, Rose felt as though she'd known the countess all her life. Lady Beatrice was sharp-witted, full of lively interest, and clearly enjoyed discussing everything from fashion to the estate. Rose suspected that her confinement made her all the more eager for company, though she found herself rather enjoying the countess's irreverent quips, especially when the topic turned to Rose's wardrobe.

"I understand your desire to mourn your father," the countess remarked as Rose helped wheel her into the dining room. "But surely a splash of color wouldn't go amiss after all this time. A deep sapphire or a ruby red, perhaps. You'd look splendid in red."

Rose recalled a gown she had once admired in a gazette—a bold red silk with tiny puffed sleeves and a scandalously low neckline. It was the sort of dress she might have chosen in her former, more rebellious life. But now, determined to be a lady, she shook her head. "I fear such colors are a bit too bold for an unmarried woman, my lady."

"Poppycock!" Lady Beatrice retorted, her eyes narrowing. "How is a young woman supposed to attract a husband if she's draped in dreary grays?

Rose wasn't quite sure how to respond. She had always prided herself on being a bit more sensible than the ton, less preoccupied with appearances. But Lady Beatrice's clear disdain for her current wardrobe left her floundering for a polite answer.

"I don't mean to dress as a sparrow, my lady," she said at last, carefully weighing her words. "But neither do I wish to appear... fast."

"Better to be fast than slow, my dear," Lady Beatrice quipped, her fingers tapping impatiently on the armrest. Then her expression softened, and she smiled. "If it's a matter of money, I'm sure Henry could advance you a bit from your salary. He mentioned your father's unfortunate disinheritance. I'd be happy to help if your purse is feeling a bit light."

Rose flushed. "It isn't the money, my lady," she murmured, embarrassed that Lady Beatrice thought her destitute. "While my father may have disinherited me, my mother left me a comfortable sum. I'm not an heiress, but I'm far from destitute."

The countess looked properly contrite. "Oh dear, I've offended you. I didn't mean to. Believe me, no one knows more than I do what it's like to have more pride than pounds. Will you forgive me?"

Rose's heart softened at the older woman's hopeful expression. "Of course, my lady," she said with a gentle smile. "And perhaps... a few new gowns wouldn't go amiss. It's been an age since I've had anything new."

"And in cheerful colors, I hope?" Lady Beatrice pressed, her eyes gleaming with excitement. "You must think me a meddling old woman, but I adore clothes! Stuck in this chair as I am, it's no fun dressing myself. But dressing you—well, that's another matter."

Rose chuckled and gave the countess's hand a light squeeze. "I'll consider it."

They were just starting the soup course when Rose remembered the earl's promise to show her the estate. "Will his lordship be joining us for luncheon?" she asked, glancing out the large mullioned windows.

Lady Beatrice gave a delicate sniff. "I wouldn't know," she said, raising her spoon. "I'm only his mother, and he seldom sees fit to inform me of his plans."

Before Rose could respond, the door to the dining room swung open, and Lord Ashbourne entered, looking every bit the rugged countryman in mud-splattered boots and well-worn riding clothes.

"My apologies, Mother. Miss Sheffield," he greeted them, pressing a kiss to Lady Beatrice's cheek. "We had some trouble with the north field. Seepage from last night's rain. Took us all morning to drain it."

Lady Beatrice shot a pointed look at his boots. "You should consult Mr. Clark," she suggested, before turning her attention back to her meal. "Your father always trusted him."

"I might," Henry replied thoughtfully. "I'd forgotten he was back at the home farm."

"After luncheon, you'll take Miss Sheffield for a ride," Lady Beatrice interjected firmly. "Let Lucien deal with Mr. Clark. The boy does little enough to earn his salary."

Henry scowled but said nothing. Rose, watching the exchange, felt a pang of sympathy for him. It was clear his mother kept him firmly under her thumb, a feeling Rose knew all too well from her own experiences with her father.

"If you're too busy, my lord, I understand," Rose offered, hoping to ease the tension. "There will be other days, surely."

Instead of appreciating her attempt at diplomacy, Henry shot her a dark look. "As I had already planned to show you the estate, Miss Sheffield, there's no need to wait." His voice was cool, his eyes unreadable. "Shall we say twenty minutes after luncheon?"

"That will be fine, my lord," Rose replied stiffly, inwardly vowing never to offer an olive branch again. It was just as she'd suspected: trying to be a lady was a thankless task.

Chapter Seven

After luncheon, Henry retreated to his study for a quick review of the estate accounts, while Miss Sheffield went up to her room to change. He was scanning over his tenants' payments when the sound of wheels turning caught his attention. His mother, escorted by a footman, maneuvered her chair through the door with a look of playful accusation in her bright green eyes.

"Aha! I knew I'd find you hiding in here," she scolded, fixing him with an exaggeratedly disapproving frown. "What do you mean by holing up in your study like a hermit when you promised to take Miss Sheffield riding?"

"I'm simply waiting for Miss Sheffield to join me, Mother," Henry replied, though guilt crept up his spine, as it always did when he saw her in that damned chair—a reminder of his failure that weighed on him like a millstone.

"She's quite the lively thing," Lady Beatrice remarked, dismissing the footman with a casual wave of her hand. "A bit naive in her notions, perhaps, but I must say, I like her much more than any of the others. Thank you for bringing her to me."

Henry set down the papers and crossed the room to stand beside her chair. "You know this is only temporary," he warned gently, hating the thought of snatching away her newfound happiness. "As soon as I find you a proper companion, Miss Sheffield will be off to join her great-aunt in Aberdeen."

"Perhaps. But that could take weeks," Lady Beatrice mused, her lips curving into a sly smile. "And even if you do find another silly girl to take the post, I see no reason why Miss Sheffield can't remain here as a guest. Couldn't she?"

Henry considered his mother's suggestion. While he had long since forgiven Miss Sheffield for her rather unorthodox greeting with the bed warmer, he wasn't sure he was prepared to make her a permanent fixture in his life. "That's true," he conceded with a sigh. "But I think we should wait before making any suggestions. She may have other plans, or her great-aunt might not permit her to stay."

"Poppycock," Lady Beatrice scoffed, waving away his objections. "I'm sure Charlotte would be thrilled to have the child remain with us. Now, where are you planning to take her?"

"I thought I'd show her the North Fields, near the old Roman ruins," he replied, resigned to his mother's usual way of changing subjects. He had learned long ago not to argue when she had set her mind on something.

"Excellent," Lady Beatrice nodded approvingly. "From our brief conversation, I gathered she's a bit of a bluestocking. I'm sure she'll appreciate the history. Perhaps you could even translate some of the inscriptions for her? You did take honors in Latin, after all," she added with a touch of maternal pride that made Henry smile.

His time at Oxford had been bittersweet, the solace of his books and studies overshadowed by painful memories outside the classroom. His smile faded, replaced by the familiar sting of old humiliations.

The sound of the door opening brought him back to the present. He looked up just as Miss Sheffield entered, her cheeks flushed and breath a little hurried.

"I'm terribly sorry if I kept you waiting, my lord," she apologized, brushing a stray curl behind her ear. She felt self-conscious in her old riding habit, which had grown loose from the weight she'd lost over the last year. It had taken all of Maggie's skills to alter it into something resembling fashionable.

"Not at all, Miss Sheffield," he replied, his deep voice betraying none of the pleasure her appearance stirred within him. Her riding habit, made of mulberry serge trimmed with gold and black braid, flattered her delicate figure beautifully. The velvet hat, with its black veil and curling feather, framed her face in a way that made her look completely enchanting.

"What a charming habit, my dear!" Lady Beatrice exclaimed, clapping her hands together. "Did I not tell you brighter colors would suit you?"

"Yes, my lady," Rose murmured, warmth flooding her cheeks under the countess's praise and the subtle admiration she caught in the earl's gaze. "I know it's not quite proper for mourning, but—"

"Nonsense," Lady Beatrice cut in with authority. "It's perfectly lovely. And as it's unlikely you and Ashbourne will encounter anything other than sheep on your ride, propriety can take a rest. Off with you both." She gave Henry a stern look. "And don't bring her back until she's got roses in her cheeks. She's far too pale.

Half an hour later, Henry and Rose rode together across the green hills, the cool, damp wind stinging their faces. When they reached the crest of a rise, Rose pulled her horse to a stop and turned to Henry with a breathless laugh of sheer delight.

"I do hope your mother will be satisfied with these roses in my cheeks, my lord," she teased, momentarily forgetting her reserve as the exhilaration of the ride took hold of her. "I feel as though my face is frozen solid!"

Henry leaned forward in his saddle, the reins held loosely in his hands, his gaze fixed on her flushed, glowing features. "Shall we turn back then?" he asked, trying to sound the dutiful host, though something in him didn't want the moment to end.

"Heaven, no!" Rose exclaimed, her laughter ringing out once more, her eyes sparkling with a playful glint. "I was only jesting, my lord. I assure you, I'm thoroughly enjoying myself. Please, let's continue."

Relief surged in Henry's chest, though he refused to acknowledge it. He inclined his head, his lips twitching into a rare smile. "Very well. There are some ruins just beyond the next hill," he said, gesturing with his riding crop. "They're said to be Roman, though I have my doubts."

"Oh, how exciting," Rose said eagerly, remembering the ruins she had visited near Colchester on holiday with her father. She had been utterly captivated by the idea of standing where emperors had once walked and had thrown herself into researching the history of the Romans. She gave Henry a sidelong glance, her curiosity piqued.

Less than ten minutes later, they stood before a massive column of weathered marble, the stone stained black from centuries of exposure. Rose ran her gloved fingers over the deep grooves carved into the ancient surface, marveling at the sheer size and age of the structure. "Why do you doubt they're Roman?" she asked, glancing at him with inquisitive eyes. "They look much like the other ruins I've seen. And that's Latin." She pointed toward the arch above.

quicken. Yes, she thought, biting her lip, the wild danger was all too obvious where he was concerned.

They resumed their ride, the tension between them simmering just beneath the surface. As they neared the manor once more, Rose found herself stealing glances at him, noticing the way the wind tugged at his dark hair, the way his broad shoulders seemed to fill the space around him. He was a man of contrasts—both lord and farmer, scholar and brute—and the realization unsettled her more than she cared to admit.

Within a week of her arrival, Rose felt as though she had always been a part of Thornfield Manor. She and the countess had quickly become fast friends, and Rose relished every moment in Lady Beatrice's company. Unlike many invalids Rose had encountered, Lady Beatrice refused to wallow in her infirmities, instead remaining surprisingly cheerful. Not that she was all sweetness and light, of course. Lady Beatrice was sharp-witted, with a tongue to match, keeping Rose entertained with her wry observations about the world—and, often, about her own son.

The countess also manipulated her brooding son with an almost artful combination of helplessness and hectoring, which left Rose wide-eyed with admiration. Where Rose had always considered her own tendency to influence others as unladylike, the countess demonstrated that a woman could wield power in the most delicate of ways and still be regarded as the epitome of refinement. For someone like Rose, who had vowed to become a true lady no matter the cost, Lady Beatrice's example was a revelation.

While Rose's mornings were devoted to the countess, her afternoons were her own. Lady Beatrice napped during this time, and Rose either read or explored the vast, elegant house. One afternoon, as she stood in the grand library, studying the portraits of the earl's ancestors, she was startled by the sound of footsteps. She turned to find Lord Ashbourne entering the room.

"A smug-looking lot, aren't they?" Henry's deep voice drawled from behind her. He was smiling as he gazed up at the portrait of a dark-haired man clad in velvet and lace. "Lords of all they surveyed."

"Lords of this place, certainly." Rose's gaze shifted from the features on the canvas to the man standing behind her. He had just come in from the fields, smelling of sweet hay and horses, a scent that stirred something in her chest. That she should notice such a personal detail unnerved her, and she turned back to the portraits to cover her confusion.

"And whom might this gentleman be?" she asked, determined to keep her tone light. "He looks like quite the fierce fellow."

Henry's eyes followed hers to the portrait she indicated. "That's my grandfather, the fifth Earl of Ashbourne."

Rose studied the dark hair and the cold, remote expression of the man in the painting. "You favor him," she said quietly, recalling the first time she had seen Henry looming in her doorway, all imposing height and stern features.

He lifted an eyebrow, his eyes gleaming with amusement. "Do I? That's hardly a compliment, you know. They called him the Black Beast of Thornfield, as much for his temper as his appearance. I'm sad to say I resemble him in that as well."

The dryness in his tone made Rose smile. "I have noticed how the household quakes in fear of your fierce temper," she teased, recalling how Mabel had scolded him that morning for tracking mud into his mother's sitting room.

Henry chuckled, his gaze softening as he looked at her. "Ah, yes, the terror of Thornfield indeed."

Rose's eyes were caught by another portrait, a young woman with golden hair and blue eyes. "And who is this?" she asked, moving closer to study the painting. "She's lovely."

An indulgent smile softened Henry's face. "That's my grandmother—the lady who tamed the beast," he said, his voice warm with affection. "She died when I was a child, but I remember her playing the pianoforte. I believe she was quite talented."

Rose felt a pang of nostalgia. "My mother played as well," she said, her voice tinged with sadness. "But I can't recall that she did so with any great ability." She forced a smile, hoping to shake off the bittersweet memory. "In that, my lord, I am said to resemble her."

Henry's green eyes sparkled with amusement. "Do you mean to say you're not a gifted musician, Miss Sheffield?" he teased. "I must confess, I'm disappointed. I thought all proper young ladies excelled at music and watercolors."

Rose's amusement faded, replaced by a sharp pang of bitterness. She turned back to the portrait, her voice suddenly tight. "A proper young lady, my lord, would never dream of excelling at anything," she said with a forced laugh. "To do so might lead to her being labeled intelligent—or worse, intellectual. And you must know that would never do."

Henry frowned, the playful atmosphere between them dissipating. "Why not?" he asked, his tone serious now. "Better to be considered clever than foolish, I should think."

"That's because you're a man," she replied, her voice edged with frustration. "A man is expected to have a brain and is granted leave to use it. But if a woman does the same, it's considered an impropriety. Men will shake their heads at her, call her a bluestocking, and she'll find herself on the shelf before she's even had a chance."

Henry's expression darkened, and he drew himself up to his full height. "I think you're being rather unfair in your assessment of men, Miss Sheffield," he said, his voice cool. "Men aren't the only ones who pass judgment. Women are equally guilty of labeling others."

"That may be," Rose shot back, her cheeks flushing with temper. "But a man can wear his reputation like a badge of honor. A woman, on the other hand, will find her reputation ruined for the same behavior."

Henry's jaw clenched, his eyes flashing with icy anger. "If you truly believe that, Miss Sheffield, then you are more foolish than I imagined," he bit out, his voice as cold as winter frost. "Now, if you'll excuse me, I must go and change. Good day to you."

With that, he turned on his heel and left the room, leaving Rose glaring after him, her heart pounding in the aftermath of their heated exchange.

Three days after their confrontation, Rose sat in the countess's study, a pile of letters spread out before her. Lady Beatrice maintained correspondence with what seemed like half the ton, and one of Rose's duties was to help sort through the daily post. She had just handed one letter to the countess and was in the process of opening another when she heard Lady Beatrice sigh heavily.

"Is something amiss, my lady?" Rose asked, glancing up from the letter in her hands.

"No, no, nothing of consequence." Lady Beatrice set the letter aside with another sigh. "It's from my dear friend, Lady Amberley. She's returning to Derbyshire next week and wishes to call on me."

"I see," Rose replied, unsure of the source of the countess's distress. "Would you like me to write a letter of regret, my lady?"

"What? No, no," Lady Beatrice shook her head. "I'm quite looking forward to seeing Harriet again. It's just..." Her voice trailed off, and she picked up her teacup, staring into its depths.

"It's just what, my lady?" Rose prompted gently.

"It's just that Harriet is bringing her nieces and a friend with her," Lady Beatrice said, her voice filled with foreboding. "And it's not me they're interested in meeting—it's Henry. Harriet means to introduce them to my son, and I'm afraid that's quite impossible."

Rose frowned. "But why?" she asked, thoroughly puzzled. "Shouldn't you be grateful that Lady Amberley wishes to introduce his lordship to eligible young ladies? There can't be many marriageable women in this part of Derbyshire."

"That's exactly the problem!" Lady Beatrice clasped her hands in agitation. "There are only a handful of young ladies left who don't swoon at the mere mention of Henry's name, and now Harriet is bringing two more to tea! If Henry frightens them off, as he has with all the others, what will become of him? He'll die a bachelor, and the line will die with him!"

The countess's distress left Rose momentarily speechless. It had never occurred to her that men could suffer the same pressure from their families to marry as women did. The realization struck her as highly amusing, but it was clear Lady Beatrice did not share her sentiment, so she wisely kept her humor to herself.

"I understand your concern, my lady," Rose said carefully, "but if the earl has no interest in these ladies, won't he remain unmarried regardless?"

"Perhaps," Lady Beatrice conceded, looking so unhappy that Rose's heart went out to her. "But I was hoping I could make him more... acceptable. You must agree, no lady in her right mind would marry him as he is now."

"My lady!" Rose stared at her in astonishment. The countess's harsh words reminded her of the arguments she had had with her own father, and it hurt her to think that Lady Beatrice could speak so callously of her son.

Seeing Rose's stunned expression, Lady Beatrice flushed. "Now you think I'm the most unnatural mother alive," she murmured, her eyes misting with tears. "And I suppose you're right. But I worry about Henry. I want him to be happy. I want him to marry. And he never will if he keeps behaving so... churlishly."

The countess's tears softened Rose's heart, even though she was still somewhat miffed with Henry. "I haven't observed his lordship behaving with any real impropriety," she lied, avoiding Lady Beatrice's piercing gaze.

"Oh, come now," Lady Beatrice scoffed. "You knocked him out with a bed warmer within seconds of meeting him. Laid him flat, according to Mabel."

Rose flushed with embarrassment. "He forced his way into my room! What else was I supposed to do?"

"I'm not condemning you, my dear." Lady Beatrice waved away her protest. "You behaved as any lady might under similar circumstances. But my point is, Henry had no right to force his way into your room. And that brutish conduct is exactly why he's so unsuitable as a suitor. Can you imagine how a delicately bred young lady would respond to such provocation? She'd faint dead away! And any hope I have of marrying him off would vanish."

"Perhaps," Rose conceded, remembering Miss Masterson's reaction to the earl. "But I still think you're worrying too much, my lady. And besides, what can you do about it? The earl is a grown man. He's hardly likely to change his ways at this late stage."

Lady Beatrice's eyes sparkled with cunning as she leaned closer. "Exactly. Which is why we—you and I—must change them for him."

Chapter Eight

Lord, was he exhausted. Henry brushed the damp hair from his forehead as he wearily ascended the front steps leading to the house. It had been a hellish day—filled with backbreaking, frustrating work—and all he wanted was to bolt down supper and crawl into bed. He was even contemplating forgoing food altogether when the door opened, and his butler greeted him with a bow.

Henry stopped mid-step, a frown pulling his brows together as he studied the older man. Williams had been with him only a short while, but Henry knew the butler thought entirely too much of his own importance to answer the door like a common footman. That he was doing so now boded ill, and Henry sighed, resigning himself to the fact that his hope for a quiet evening was about to be dashed. "What is it, Williams?" he asked heavily, silently bidding farewell to the peaceful evening he'd been craving.

"Her ladyship and Miss Sheffield are waiting for you in the drawing room, my lord," Williams intoned, his face impeccably blank despite Henry's disheveled appearance. "They asked that you join them there."

Henry bit back an oath. "Now?" He made no effort to hide his displeasure.

Williams raised a single bushy eyebrow, arching it with the kind of cool disdain only an experienced butler could muster. "I am sure her ladyship would understand if you wish to change first, my lord," he offered with a sniff. "Shall I inform her you will be with her shortly?"

Henry glanced down at his dusty jacket and grass-stained breeches. He was in no state to grace anything other than a stable. He opened his mouth to agree, but then something stubborn and rebellious took hold of him. The devil take it, he thought, his lips thinning with impatience. If his mother and Miss Sheffield were so eager to see him, then he'd be happy to oblige them—filthy as he was.

"The drawing room, did you say?"

"Yes, my lord," Williams replied, his features stiffening, the barest hint of anxiety flashing across them. "However, I feel I should—" The butler cut himself off, resignation in his eyes as Henry stalked past him.

The drawing room door was closed, and Henry pushed it open with an impatient shove, his jaw set as he braced for whatever awaited him. Inside, his mother and Miss Sheffield sat beside a roaring fire, the warmth of the room a stark contrast to the tension simmering within him.

"You wished to see me, Mother?" His voice was cool, and he made no move to approach them further.

If Lady Beatrice noticed his sullen tone, she didn't show it. Instead, she beamed at him, her eyes alight with disguised pleasure. "Oh, Henry, there you are!" she exclaimed happily, holding out her arms as if welcoming a conquering hero. "Stop hovering in the doorway and come greet your mother properly! I haven't seen you in days!"

THE BEASTLY EARL AND HIS ROSE

A pang of guilt shot through Henry at her enthusiasm. He pushed himself away from the door, his annoyance momentarily checked. "You saw me yesterday," he reminded her, though his smile softened as he stepped forward to kiss her cheek. She looked healthier, less pale than she had recently, and the realization eased some of his frustration.

"Yes, I saw you," Lady Beatrice returned with a pretty pout, "but all you offered were a few words before dashing off. Had it not been for dear Rose, I would have been left to converse with the syllabub!"

The image of his mother talking earnestly to a dessert dish made Henry's lips twitch in amusement. "My apologies, Mother, but as I told you, Lady Townes was foaling, and—"

"Yes, yes, I know," she interrupted, waving his explanation away with a graceful hand. "And I'm not precisely scolding you, am I, dearest?" She turned to her companion, seeking confirmation

"Indeed you are not, my lady," Rose assured her with a conspiratorial smile.

"There, you see?" Lady Beatrice shot Henry a triumphant look and patted the settee beside her. "Now sit and tell us how you've spent your day. You've clearly been among the cows, if your attire is any indication."

Before replying, Henry accepted the tea and plate of delicacies Miss Sheffield handed him. "We moved the herd to the north pasture," he began, unsure how much detail was appropriate for a lady's ears. "The calves have all been delivered, and it's time we began fattening them for market. If prices hold, we'll make a tidy profit by autumn."

"How wonderful!" His mother beamed with pride. "Did I tell you my son was brilliant?" she demanded of Rose, her smug tones making Henry distinctly uncomfortable. "He knows exactly what he's about."

"He certainly seems quite competent," Rose replied, casting Henry a teasing smile that sent an unexpected thrill through him. "What will your lordship do once the animals and crops are all tended to?" she asked, her tone warm with interest. "Will you go to London?"

Henry winced at the suggestion. "Lord, no," he muttered, recalling his last miserable visit to the city. "The only reason any sane man would go there would be to attend Parliament, and as the session ends next week, I see no reason to bother. Besides," he added, the thought suddenly striking him, "with the Season ending, everyone will have returned to the country."

His mother and Rose exchanged a knowing look, and Lady Beatrice picked up her teacup, her tone bright with mischief. "How interesting you should mention that," she began, making Henry instantly suspicious. "You'll never guess who has written to me... Harriet!"

"Harriet who?" he asked, though he suspected where this was heading.

"Now, Henry, don't be obtuse." She frowned at him. "You know perfectly well I'm referring to my dear friend, Lady Amberley."

"Ah, yes." Henry managed not to shudder at the thought of the witless countess. "And how is she?"

"As well as can be expected, considering her age," Lady Beatrice replied, conveniently forgetting that Lady Amberley was only three years her junior. "She arrives home next week, and I thought it would be nice to have her over for tea. With your permission, of course."

"Mother—" Henry set his cup aside and took her hand in his. "You know you may invite anyone you please. This is your home, after all."

"Of course, I know that, dearest." She squeezed his hand gently. "But the last time I had guests, you were so distant that they left highly insulted. Harriet is one of my oldest friends, and I don't want to subject her or her guests to similar treatment. I thought it best to ask your permission."

Henry flushed at the rebuke. He remembered that particular incident all too well. He had tried to be pleasant to the young ladies in question, but they had reacted as if he meant to ravish them on the spot. One had even swooned when he'd merely offered to show her the orangery.

The memory soured his mood, but as he looked into his mother's hopeful eyes, he couldn't bring himself to refuse her. What sort of son would he be to deny her this small pleasure?

"Invite whomever you like, Mother," he said softly, lifting her hand to his lips. "I promise I'll be the soul of charm."

His mother smiled, her lashes fluttering. "Very well," she said meekly. "If you're sure you don't mind."

"Not at all," he lied. "In fact, I'm sure Miss Sheffield will welcome the company as well."

Rose met his gaze, amusement dancing in her eyes. "Company is always a welcome diversion, my lord," she said, her tone deceptively mild, but the sparkle in her eyes made it clear she saw straight through him.

"Well then, that's settled!" Lady Beatrice clapped her hands together, her eyes sparkling with excitement. "Rose, be a dear and ring for the footman."

"Certainly, my lady." Rose did as asked, then offered, "Shall I accompany you upstairs?"

"Heavens, no!" Lady Beatrice laughed. "I can't compose a single word with someone hovering over me. You stay here with his lordship. I'm sure the two of you have plenty to discuss."

Henry shot Rose a considering look. She seemed surprisingly unperturbed by the idea of being left alone with him. Most unmarried women of his acquaintance would be scandalized by the notion. It struck him as suspicious that his usually propriety-obsessed mother would leave them unchaperoned. His eyes gleamed with curiosity.

Once his mother had been escorted from the room, Henry turned to Rose, amusement tugging at his lips. "Subtlety has never been one of Mother's strengths," he remarked. "I hope you don't mind?"

Rose smiled, relieved he wasn't offended by Lady Beatrice's scheming. "Not at all, my lord. I only hope you're not offended by her... obviousness."

"Not in the least," he said, his voice softening as his gaze lingered on her. "I assume my devious mother is up to something." His gaze met her in unmistakable challenge. "have you any idea what that something might be?

Rose set her teacup aside, accepting the challenge with alacrity. "As a matter of fact, I believe I do," she said, her voice smooth. "Lady Beatrice is looking forward to Lady Amberley's visit, but she felt the prospect of company is not to your liking. Is that true?"

Henry was taken aback by the bold demand. "What nonsense," he muttered, scowling as he glanced away. "You heard what I said to my mother, Miss Sheffield. I have no objections to visitors. She may invite whomever she pleases."

"Having no objection is hardly a glowing testament, my lord." Rose tried not to wince at the guilt pricking her as she delivered the carefully rehearsed speech she and the countess had prepared. "Your mother is afraid you'll be miserable with a house full of guests, and she's willing to sacrifice her happiness to guarantee your own."

"But that's ridiculous!" Henry protested, clearly appalled by the news. "I've told her a dozen times that I—" His voice trailed off as suspicion flickered in his eyes. "A house full of guests?" he repeated slowly. "I thought we were talking about Lady Amberley coming over for tea."

"And so we were," Rose agreed with a nod, keeping her tone composed. "But your mother has been saying how much she longs to see her old friends again. Since she can't travel anymore, it makes far more sense for them to come to her, don't you agree?"

Henry rose from his seat and began to pace, his restless energy palpable. "Of course, I agree," he said with a sigh, running a hand through his dark hair. The strands fell in disarray around his collar, making him look even more untamed. "It's just…"

"Just what, my lord?" Rose pressed gently, not missing the flicker of vulnerability in his expression.

Henry paused in front of the mirror above the mantel, his reflection grim. The day's exertions had left his hair untidy, and the rough, work-worn jacket he wore only added to the impression of a man more suited to the wild than polite society. His lips curled in a bitter smile. The Ox from Oxford, they had called him. What would his mother's guests say if they saw him now? He turned from the mirror in disgust.

"It's just that both you and my mother are right," he admitted at last, his gaze dropping to the floor. "I'm uncomfortable with strangers, but that doesn't mean she should suffer for my faults." He raised his eyes to meet Rose's, something raw flickering in their depths. "Please assure her I want her to invite as many people as she pleases. I'll manage."

Rose could see the weight of his discomfort, the sincerity in his words, and it softened something within her. But her task wasn't finished. "I can tell her anything you wish, sir," she replied carefully, "but I doubt it will do much good. Unless your mother sees you truly act as if you're comfortable with guests, she's unlikely to invite anyone at all."

Henry frowned. "What do you mean?"

"I mean," Rose said, summoning every ounce of composure, "that words alone won't convince her. If you really wish to put her at ease, you'll need to show her—convincingly—that you don't mind a house full of guests."

"And how exactly am I supposed to manage that?" he demanded, frustration simmering in his voice. He cursed himself for being the reason his mother had gone without company for so long.

Rose busied herself refilling their cups, her heart squeezing at the sight of the inner turmoil clouding his eyes. Whatever caused his wariness around people, she realized it wasn't mere caprice. The temptation to abandon her plan and offer him comfort instead rose within her, but she couldn't bear the thought of disappointing the countess. She pressed on, forcing herself to remain composed as she handed him his tea.

"Lady Amberley arrives within the week," she began carefully. "Perhaps in the meantime, you might make more of an effort to socialize. A ride into town, or inviting a few friends over, would be a good start. You do have friends, don't you?" she added hastily, her eyes widening as if the possibility that he might not crossed her mind for the first time.

Despite his dark mood, Henry couldn't help but smile at her sudden concern. "I'm not so much of a monster that I've driven everyone away," he assured her dryly. "Sebastian Westwood lives but a mile or so from here. He's in London for Parliament, but I do have several good friends."

Rose relaxed, though the tension between them remained electric. "And what of your neighbors?" she pressed, hoping to keep the conversation moving forward. The thought struck her unexpectedly: If only he smiled more, the house would be overrun with eager ladies, all desperate to catch his attention.

Henry thought of the local vicar and his wife, their usual guests when formality dictated. It was an option, but not one that filled him with any enthusiasm. Still, if it would help his mother, he could suffer through their company again. "The vicar, perhaps," he mused. "And Squire Seeley. There's a section of his land I've been meaning to discuss—"

"No," Rose interrupted, shaking her head firmly. "The taking of tea is a social occasion, my lord. If your mother suspects you've invited the squire to talk about farming, we'll be right back where we started."

He gritted his teeth, knowing she was right. "Very well, then. Who else would you suggest?"

"We need more than just four people," Rose replied with a decisive air, her mind racing. "And, of course, we'll need unattached ladies and gentlemen to round out the numbers. Do you know any eligible candidates?"

Henry wanted to suggest they abandon the whole charade, but he could see there was no backing out now. "The Hartfords have several daughters," he said at last, his tone resigned. "They're supposed to be stunners, and they stayed home this Season due to mourning."

"Stunners, you say?" Rose repeated, trying to ignore the strange pang that shot through her at the thought of these so-called 'stunners' invading Thornfield. She imagined the house teeming with elegant, accomplished women, all angling for Ashbourne's attention, and a wave of something sharp and unwelcome settled in her chest.

She wondered suddenly, would anyone ever call her a stunner? Somehow, she doubted it. Her reputation as a headstrong woman had followed her for so long that it often overshadowed anything else. And yet, the notion gnawed at her, despite herself—would the earl ever think of her that way?

The question hit her like a blow, unsettling her to the core. The mere possibility that she might care about his opinion shook her, and she quickly buried the thought as she turned her gaze back to him. But the answer lingered, teasing her as much as the tension between them.

"Who else?" she asked, her voice a little too bright, desperate to move on from the dangerous path her thoughts had taken.

Henry was about to snap that he was hardly a matchmaking mama who kept tabs on every eligible man in the county, when a name suddenly surfaced.

"Nate!" he exclaimed, his green eyes sparking with an energy that made Rose pause, taking note of the change in his expression.

"Who?"

"The Honorable Nathaniel Langford, younger son of the Earl of Eastwick," Henry explained, already beginning to enjoy the prospect of his home filling with guests. "He's based in Derby when he's not in London, and I remember him saying he'd be returning early. If he's back, he'll be more than happy to attend. In fact, Nate's always surrounded by young bucks eager to trail after him. Shall I write to him?"

"If you would, my lord," Rose replied, though there was a tightness in her chest. She hadn't anticipated her own reaction to the thought of Thornfield being overrun by such men. The very idea of a house filled with Nate Langford's fashionable, rakish friends unsettled her, though she couldn't quite understand why. The earl gave her a curious look, sensing something more.

"Is there anything else, Miss Sheffield?" Henry's sharp gaze didn't miss much. "Shall I also see to the refreshments?"

She tossed her head back, trying to hide her growing unease. "The Countess and I shall manage the food," she replied tartly. "All we require from you is your presence."

"There must be more," Henry pressed, his eyes narrowing in on her discomfort. "Come now, Miss Sheffield, spit it out. I promise not to fly off the handle."

Rose hesitated, but the intensity of his stare made it impossible to back down. "It's... your clothing," she finally blurted, her voice trembling ever so slightly. Her cheeks flushed with the heat of embarrassment, but there was no turning back now. "You'll forgive me, I hope, but I couldn't help but notice that you..."

"That I what?" Henry's tone sharpened, the playful gleam in his eyes vanishing as he set his cup down and folded his arms across his chest. His broad chest. "Don't stop now, Miss Sheffield. What is it about my wardrobe that leaves you so speechless? The color? Or perhaps the cut?"

Rose swallowed hard. "It's everything, if you must know," she snapped, deciding that the arrogant brute didn't deserve her restraint. "The first thing I noticed about you was how poorly your clothes fit—years out of fashion. Indeed, the only thing you own that's remotely appropriate is your riding attire, and you can hardly wear that to tea!"

Henry's eyes flashed with fury, his posture growing more rigid. "Indeed?" His voice was frigid. "Then perhaps you're not as au courant as you think. According to the latest issue of Le Beau Monde, wearing one's riding togs in the drawing room is all the rage!"

Rose shot back without thinking. "Perhaps, but only if the jackets are properly tailored and don't look as though they're about to burst at the seams!"

The words tumbled out before she could stop them, and as her gaze lingered on him, she couldn't help but notice the way his coat strained across the broad expanse of his back and shoulders. It wasn't just the cut of the fabric, she realized. It was him—the raw, powerful size of him. His arms, thick with muscle from working the land, filled the sleeves in a way that no fashionable tailoring could possibly contain. There was something deeply masculine about it, a heat that made her stomach flutter, and she quickly averted her eyes, chastising herself for such an unladylike reaction.

"Oh dear," she whispered, the weight of her thoughtlessness crashing over her. "What a dreadful cat you must think me. I didn't mean... I'm sorry, my lord."

Henry's anger ebbed, seeing the remorse in her eyes. "It is I who should apologize," he said quietly, his voice softened. "I promised I wouldn't take offense, and yet here I am, snapping at you when you were only giving the opinion I asked for."

"Yes, but I was unnecessarily cruel," Rose admitted, still burning with shame. "I hate it when people snipe at me, regardless of whether or not I've asked for their opinion. I only hope I haven't hurt you beyond repair."

She tilted her head, her expression so contrite, so earnest, that Henry couldn't help but smile despite himself. "I'm not offended, Miss Sheffield," he said, the edges of his mouth lifting in a reluctant grin as he reached for his teacup once more.

"Good," she sighed, her relief palpable as she turned her attention to her own tea.

A moment passed in silence before Henry leaned forward, mischief dancing in his eyes. "So, what are you planning to do about it?"

"Pardon?"

"My wardrobe, Miss Sheffield." His tone was all teasing now, enjoying her look of confusion. "After that scathing critique, I can only assume you've come prepared with a solution."

Rose's cheeks flamed again, but she wasn't about to let him have the last word. "Not precisely, my lord," she stammered, her blush deepening at his smug expression. "Though I was going to suggest you ask Mr. Langford for the name of his tailor. If he lives in London, he'll surely know what's fashionable."

Henry chuckled, thinking of Nate's perfectly tailored wardrobe. "Oh yes, Nate is quite the dandy, but I hardly think a London tailor will do us much good out here."

"Perhaps not, but surely he knows someone in Derby," Rose said, eager to keep the conversation moving. "We'll need to act quickly if we hope to have you properly fitted by next week."

Henry arched a brow. "Next week?"

"For the tea," she reminded him, her tone more authoritative now that they were back on track. "I was thinking Wednesday afternoon, if that suits?"

He gave her a mockingly solemn look. "Oh? Do I actually get a say in this matter?"

"Of course," she replied with a scolding tone, meeting his teasing head-on. "If Wednesday doesn't suit, we can move it to Thursday."

Henry's lips twitched, but he kept his composure. "Wednesday is fine," he said, his voice deliberately serious. "Any particular time on Wednesday, or shall I simply wait by the door in case I'm needed?"

Rose threw him a suspicious glance but couldn't help laughing. "Two o'clock," she said firmly. "And I would also appreciate it if you made yourself available for the next few afternoons."

"Available?" He raised a brow. "For what exactly?"

"For your fittings, of course," she replied, as if speaking to a child. "The moment we learn the name of Mr. Langford's tailor, I plan to send for him at once. The sooner you're fitted for your new wardrobe, the better."

Chapter Nine

Two days later, Rose was hard at work in the study Lady Beatrice had set aside for her use. The tea party had somehow morphed into a garden party, and the guest list had swelled to include nearly thirty people. Worse, it showed no signs of stopping. She'd tried mentioning her concerns, but the older woman had simply waved them off with a laugh.

"Nonsense, child! What is one person more or less?" Lady Beatrice had said, her tone as carefree as her smile. "As my mother-in-law used to say, it's better to invite everyone than risk offending anybody. Just see to it, my dear, and all will be fine."

Rose wasn't so sure. Lady Beatrice's optimism might be unshakable, but Rose was beginning to experience serious doubts about her ability to pull everything together in time. The staff was wonderful, thankfully, and even seemed to welcome the challenge of preparing the house. Even Lord Ashbourne was cooperating—for him. Rather than wasting time on a letter, he'd ridden into Derby to visit his friend and returned not only with the name of Mr. Langford's tailor but also with a new valet, a small, delicately built man who went by the name of Samuels. Samuels, formerly employed by a renowned dandy, had solemnly assured Rose that it would be his personal mission to "bring his lordship up to snuff."

The weather was cooperating as well. The cool, damp days had given way to warm sunlight and soft summer breezes, and the garden was a riot of roses and pinks. Gazing out the window at the vibrant blooms, Rose had to admit, things were going remarkably well.

Except for one thing. And it had nothing to do with the house, the guests, or even Lord Ashbourne.

She had been at Thornfield Manor for almost a fortnight, and aside from a few sharp exchanges with the earl, she had managed to behave with propriety. Lady Beatrice praised her endlessly, and even Mrs. Lester, the housekeeper, had remarked that she'd never seen a sweeter young lady. But propriety was something Rose had always struggled with. Would she be able to maintain her carefully constructed facade once there were more people about? Or would she revert to her old ways, shocking everyone with her quick tongue and unbearable frankness?

It wasn't that she meant to misbehave. It was just that she had never been able to twist herself into the mold society demanded of a proper young lady. Her father had raised her as he might have a son, and it wasn't until her late teens that she'd realized most people found her behavior unacceptable. Learning she was regarded as a "quiz" had stung, and in response, she'd behaved even more outrageously, delighting in her well-deserved reputation.

But in the end, she had paid the price for her defiance. Invitations had grown fewer in the last year, and with the exception of Lady Catherine Clare and the new Duchess of Tilton, she had no true friends. Even her father had turned against her, condemning her for the very traits he had once instilled. That hurt more than anything. She couldn't bear it if the same thing happened here.

Her forehead pressed against the cool windowpane, she tried to shake off her melancholy when a loud commotion snapped her attention back. At first, she thought the noise was coming from outside, but then she realized it was from above. Frowning, she moved to the door and peered into the hall just in time to see the earl's newly hired tailor rushing down the stairs, his face a picture of outrage.

"Never have I been so insulted!" he raged, his voice carrying through the house. "The townsfolk are right! The man is a monster! A barbarian! A Philistine! I will not squander my talents on such a brute!"

It took Rose less than a second to realize what was happening. She darted out, lifting her skirts and rushing after him. "Monsieur! Wait! Please, don't go!" she called, breathless.

At the bottom of the stairs, the tailor turned, his face flushed with indignation. "I have sewn for kings!" he declared, dramatically shaking his tape measure at her. "For emperors! I have survived revolutions, wars, and the *dreadful* winter of London, but I will not survive another moment in that man's presence! I am leaving. Do not try to stop me!"

"What happened?" Rose hurried to intercept him, forcing herself not to laugh at the image of the earl terrorizing the poor man. "I'm sure it's all a misunderstanding—"

"I will tell you what happened," came the low, furious drawl from the staircase.

Rose looked up. There was Henry, leaning against the railing, arms crossed over his broad chest, eyes blazing. "That man wants to put me in stays," he said, the words dripping with indignation.

"They are not stays!" the tailor shot back, tossing his curls with the sort of grace a debutante might envy. "They are a device—of my own design!—to conceal the imperfections of my clients."

Rose bit her lip to keep from giggling at the image of Henry, towering and scowling, being laced into a corset. Stays, indeed.

"He is too..." The tailor gestured dramatically at his own slender frame, searching for the right words. "Too masculine to wear my designs!" He waved his hands in frustration. "His chest, it is too wide—" he patted his own thin ribcage "—and his arms, too big!" He made a sweeping motion toward his own narrow shoulders. "If I were to fit him, I would have to sacrifice the lapels! And that, mademoiselle," he said with finality, "I refuse to do!"

Rose bit the inside of her cheek, struggling to contain the laughter threatening to bubble up. "I see," she managed, her voice trembling as she fought for composure. Just then, Ashbourne descended the stairs, his expression thunderous, and she quickly realized that his mood matched the tailor's. Clearly, a compromise was necessary if she had any hope of salvaging the situation, so she forced herself to think logically.

"Perhaps you might design another jacket for his lordship?" She offered the irate tailor a hopeful smile, trying to broker peace. "One with... narrower lapels, or—"

"My jackets are renowned for their lapels!" the tailor interrupted, bristling with indignation. "To alter them by even a centimeter would be a desecration! I will not do it."

"Perhaps a modified version of your... device," Rose suggested, her tone more desperate as she prayed Ashbourne wouldn't blow up at the idea.

"I am not wearing stays like some old crone!" he snapped, crossing his arms in defiance. His white linen shirt stretched tight across his chest, drawing her attention to the breadth of his shoulders—and the flush to her cheeks.

"You see?" the tailor all but demanded, gesturing wildly with his tape measure like a battle flag. "That man has no sense of fashion! An imbecile!" He huffed, turning toward the door. "I wash my hands of him and this house!"

"Wait, monsieur! What of the earl's wardrobe?" Rose's voice pitched in desperation. "We're hosting a garden party in a few days. What shall we do for clothes?"

The tailor paused just long enough to offer her a condescending smirk. "Perhaps, mademoiselle, since you seem so intent on instructing me how to cut my jackets, you should design them yourself?" He tossed the tape measure at her feet with a dismissive flick. "You'll need this." With that, he stalked out, his beaked nose held high, leaving only the scent of his outrage behind.

"Of all the imprudence—" Ashbourne started forward, his jaw clenched as if ready to throttle the man. Rose quickly reached out, her fingers grasping his sleeve. The firm muscle beneath startled her, but she focused on calming him.

"Never mind, my lord," she sighed, resignation heavy in her voice. "There's no use trying to stop him. He's already gone."

"Stop him?" Ashbourne echoed incredulously, sending her a sharp look. "I wasn't about to stop him. I was going to help him on his way, preferably with my boot in his backside. If he ever steps foot at Thornfield Manor again, I'll have him shot!"

Rose couldn't help but share his sentiment, though she felt obliged to venture a gentle scolding. "You shouldn't be so hard on the poor man, my lord," she began in a firm tone, though her resolve wavered. "He was only trying to do his duty, and—"

Her voice faltered, and the laughter she'd been fighting finally broke free. "Stays?" she managed between giggles, her eyes sparkling as she looked up at him.

"They were sewn into the front of the jacket," Ashbourne replied, his lips twitching into a grin. "Ingenious, I'll grant him that, but damn uncomfortable. When I put that wretched thing on, I could barely draw breath." He took a step closer, his eyes dancing with mischief as he added provocatively, "Now I understand what you poor ladies endure in the name of fashion. You have my undying sympathy."

The warm tone of his voice, combined with the teasing glint in his eyes, sent a flush of awareness through her. Her fingers, still resting against the firm muscle of his arm, suddenly felt too familiar, too intimate. He was standing so close now that she could feel the heat of him, his breath a soft caress against her cheek. Her heart gave an unexpected thump.

Quickly, she dropped her hand and took a discreet step back, putting some much-needed distance between them.

"Well, it seems we're right back where we started," Rose said, keeping her tone light despite the turmoil swirling inside her. "The garden party is less than a week away, and you've not a decent shirt to your name."

Henry gave her a thoughtful look, noting the delightful flush on her cheeks and the way her eyes refused to meet his directly. He knew he should follow her lead and excuse himself, but he found himself oddly reluctant to move away. Standing this close, he could catch the soft scent of her perfume—something delicate and sweet. He allowed himself the indulgence of inhaling it before reluctantly stepping back.

"Come now, you're being unreasonably hard on my wardrobe," he teased, matching her tone. "Things aren't quite as bleak as that."

"As good as," she shot back, giving him a considering look as if only just noticing he was in his shirt sleeves. "Although, that shirt you're wearing seems adequate enough."

"Then I shall wear it and nothing else," he said, mischief gleaming in his eyes. "Perhaps I'll set a new fashion among the gentlemen."

The color in her cheeks deepened, a reaction that both frustrated and flustered her. "A short fashion, if the ladies have anything to say about it!" she snapped, furious at herself for being so affected by his boldness. "The thought of an unclothed gentleman in the parlor is not to be borne!"

"Unclothed, Miss Sheffield?" Henry repeated, his eyes widening with mock incredulity. "You shock me. I was merely suggesting I go without my jacket. Whatever did you think I meant?" He delivered the question with such innocent patience that Rose couldn't help but laugh softly.

"Wretch!" she accused, the harsh word softened by the smile on her lips. "I am serious, you know. You need new clothes."

"I don't see why," he said, taking her arm and gently guiding her into the parlor. "I have a wardrobe full of clothes I've not worn in years. Won't they do?"

"Only if you wish to be taken for a quiz," Rose countered, shaking her head. "Well, I suppose we have no choice. They'll have to suffice until we can find you another tailor."

"If he's anything like the last one, you may spare yourself the effort. I refuse to have another tulip fluttering about me."

"What do you suggest we do, then?" Rose asked, her annoyance creeping into her voice. She and Lady Beatrice had both gone to great lengths for the earl's benefit, and it seemed the least he could do was put in some effort with his appearance.

The sharpness of her tone caught Henry's attention, his brows arching in surprise. He'd been about to suggest sending for another tailor from Derby, even offering to pay double for a rush job, but now...he was hanged if he'd suggest anything at all. Instead, he lounged casually against the mantel, his manner deliberately indifferent as he gave her a cool look.

"I haven't the slightest idea, Miss Sheffield," he drawled, tossing the challenge neatly back at her. "What do you suggest?"

Her hands clenched at her sides, and Rose was wildly tempted to tell him he could take his blasted jackets and feed them to the pigs. The words hovered on her lips, ready to fly out, but she bit them back with Herculean effort. Her days of saying whatever she pleased were behind her now, she reminded herself sternly. Regardless of the temptation, she would control her tongue.

Very well, she thought, her foot tapping out an impatient rhythm as she considered the matter of the earl's wardrobe. What would she do? The garden party was looming, and a proper day coat and breeches were clearly the most pressing priority. Everything else could wait. Weighing her options, she arrived at what she believed to be the best solution for all involved.

"I suggest we have Samuels look through your wardrobe and choose the least offensive items," she said slowly, speaking aloud as she pieced together the plan. "Then we can have your mother's modiste perform whatever alterations are necessary to bring them up to current fashion." Folding her arms, she gave him a look that dared him to object. "What do you say, my lord?"

Her cleverness impressed Henry more than he cared to admit, but there was no way he was going to let her know that. Instead, he pretended to consider the notion, his mouth twisting into a thoughtful frown as he regarded her with exaggerated deliberation.

"I'm not sure I like that idea any more than I liked having that French popinjay fluttering around me," he finally said, rolling his shoulders in a casual shrug. "You'll have to think of something else."

Rose, who had fully expected him to accept her idea with suitable gratitude, scowled in annoyance. "Why should I?" she demanded. "It's the perfect solution, and you know it."

He decided to grant her that much, though he wasn't done toying with her yet. "I'm not having some half-witted seamstress taking my measurements," he stated, folding his arms as he gave her his coldest look. That look had sent grown men quaking in their boots, but he was secretly pleased to see it had no discernible effect on her. If anything, she seemed as though she'd like to hit him over the head with another bed warmer.

"Fine," she snapped, her patience fraying. "Perhaps Samuels—"

"No," he cut in, enjoying himself far too much. "He's competent enough, but it still puts me too much in mind of Monsieur André."

Rose shot him a look that dripped with scorn. "Then who do you suggest, my lord? Williams?" The idea of the stiff-necked butler performing such a task almost made Henry laugh aloud, but he kept his expression perfectly neutral.

He'd teased her long enough, and was about to agree when he noticed she was still holding the measuring tape the tailor had thrown at her. An idea bloomed in his mind, wicked and irresistible. He raised his gaze to meet hers and gave her a slow, deliberate smile.

"If you're so determined to dress me up like some simpering dandy," he drawled, his voice heavy with challenge, "then you may do the honors."

To his immense amusement, Rose turned a deep, rosy shade. "Lord Ashbourne!"

"You object?"

"Of course I object!" she sputtered, her eyes wide. "It's the most improper suggestion I've ever heard!"

"And you, naturally, would never dream of doing anything improper," he replied, nodding as if in agreement. "Very well, Miss Sheffield. As I've no wish to put you to the blush, we'll forget this conversation ever took place. If you'll excuse me, I'll return to my room." He pushed away from the mantel as though he intended to leave.

"But what about your wardrobe?" she asked, chewing her lip, her suspicion clear.

"What about it?" He shrugged with maddening indifference. "I'm not the one who finds it so objectionable. If you're unwilling to remedy the situation, then there's nothing left to say."

Rose's fingers tightened around the quill. "Your... your chest," she murmured, avoiding his eyes. This was proving even more difficult than she had anticipated, and she was strongly tempted to admit defeat. Only the knowledge that such cowardice would surely delight him kept her from doing just that, and she mentally stiffened her spine as she turned back to face him.

Taking a deep breath, she stepped closer once again, the heat of his body making her skin tingle as she wrapped the tape around his broad chest. His muscles shifted beneath her touch, and she could feel the deep rise and fall of his breath. Forcing herself to focus, Rose bit down hard on her lower lip, her thoughts dangerously close to wandering. What would it be like, she wondered, if those arms wrapped around her, if his hands—

She cut the thought short, horrified by her own imagination. With a swift movement, she yanked the tape free and hastily noted the measurement, her fingers trembling.

"There," she said, thrusting the paper toward him, her voice tight. "You may present these to the modiste."

"Are we finished so soon?" His voice was teasing, and as his fingers brushed hers while taking the paper, the touch sent an unexpected jolt through her. "What about the rest of my attire? As you've already pointed out, I can hardly make my debut in society dressed only in a shirt."

She knew exactly what he was implying. "I'm sure your valet is far more capable of finishing the task, my lord," she managed, her voice shaky despite her attempt at composure.

"More capable, perhaps," he drawled, his gaze lingering on her with that infuriating mix of mockery and something far more dangerous, "but I doubt I would enjoy it nearly as much."

Her cheeks flamed, the heat rushing through her body. She could no longer pretend it was only irritation she felt. The thought of finishing the measurements, of touching him again, of feeling his warm skin beneath her hands, was too much. It was dangerous, and it was exhilarating.

"Go to the devil," she muttered, throwing the tape at him as she backed away, desperate to escape. His rich laughter followed her, filling the room, and her pulse raced as she fled.

But as Rose hurried down the corridor, she couldn't ignore the way her heart thundered in her chest—or the realization that it wasn't anger driving her. She was running because of the undeniable pull she felt toward him, a desire so fierce it frightened her. And even as she vowed to make him pay for his mockery, part of her wondered… what if he kissed her?

The thought left her breathless, her steps faltering as she struggled to push it away. Rose pressed a hand to her heated cheek, feeling more unsettled than ever.

What on earth was happening to her?

The day of the garden party dawned cool and gray, the cheerful promise of sunshine buried beneath thick clouds that hinted at rain. Rose stood at the door, peering out into the garden with an expression as stormy as the weather. The staff had spent all of yesterday arranging tables and chairs, and the thought that their efforts might be for naught was enough to make her fists clench. Still, she brushed aside her disappointment and began plotting alternate plans should the worst occur. Perhaps they could move the festivities into the orangery...

Behind her, the soft sound of wheels squeaking across the floor signaled Lady Beatrice's arrival. The countess entered the room with her usual air of brisk command.

"Don't tell me it's raining!" Lady Beatrice exclaimed, waving the footman away with a sharp gesture.

"Not yet," Rose replied, stepping away from the window. "But it's likely to, before the afternoon is over."

Lady Beatrice gave an indignant huff. "Honestly, we often have fine weather this time of year. This is entirely your fault."

"My fault?" Rose turned, eyebrows arching at the accusation.

"Certainly. Had you invited the vicar, as Henry suggested, this would never have happened. It never does to insult God, you know."

Rose couldn't help the laugh that bubbled up. "It was you who said the man was an unmitigated bore," she pointed out, sinking into the chair at her desk. "For your information, my lady, I did invite the vicar. He and his wife will be here, along with the rest of your neighbors."

"Humph. So, we'll be preached to death and rained upon," Lady Beatrice grumbled, drumming her fingers against the arm of her chair. "I must say, this is vexing. Nothing is going as I had hoped."

The sharp words stung, and Rose glanced up from the guest list in surprise. She had worked tirelessly to ensure everything went smoothly, and she thought the preparations were coming together quite well.

The countess, noting her expression, sighed. "Oh, dear. I didn't mean to sound so critical," she offered, her tone softening. "You've done a splendid job, my dear. I'm certain it will be a success. It's not the party itself I'm worried about. It's Henry."

At the mention of his name, Rose's stomach twisted. She had been doing her best to avoid him since the *measuring incident*, but when they did cross paths, she met him with the iciest civility she could muster. He, in turn, seemed endlessly amused by her efforts—so much so that she had often longed to slap that insufferable smirk off his face.

Arrogant devil, she fumed inwardly. What had ever made her think him cold? He was a teasing, provoking beast, and she was determined to exact her revenge. Now, if only she could decide how.

Drawing herself up, she forced her expression into polite inquiry. "What of his lordship? Is there a problem with his wardrobe?"

"No, thank heavens." Lady Beatrice exhaled with relief. "His new valet has worked wonders with those dreadful old jackets. Henry hasn't looked this presentable in years." She hesitated, her fingers toying with the delicate lace at her wrist. "No, it's not his clothes I'm worried about. It's the man inside them."

Rose blinked, taken aback. Despite her current irritation with him, she admired Lord Ashbourne more than she cared to admit. It was difficult to imagine anything that might truly trouble him.

"What do you mean?" she asked, leaning forward.

Lady Beatrice sighed, her voice softening as her gaze became distant. "You don't know Henry as well as I do. He's not nearly as sanguine about this party as he pretends."

"I know he agreed to it to please you," Rose replied slowly, remembering how reluctantly the earl had initially warmed to the idea. "But he's been quite helpful since. Why, it was his suggestion to use the small tents to protect the food from the heat and insects."

"Oh, he'll do his duty," Lady Beatrice said with a humorless laugh. "Just like his father. But that doesn't mean he's looking forward to this afternoon with anything but dread."

Rose frowned. "Why?" she pressed. She knew the party might be tedious for a worldly man like Ashbourne, but something in Lady Beatrice's tone suggested there was more to it than mere boredom.

The countess hesitated, her fingers twisting together. "We never speak of it," she began cautiously, "but Henry hides himself here for a reason. There's a... tragedy in his past. He would be furious if he knew I told you, but I think you deserve to understand."

Rose braced herself, ready to hear about some dreadful scandal. A duel, perhaps? She could easily imagine the earl, cold and unflinching, facing down an opponent with a pistol in hand. Or perhaps an affair? Yes, that seemed likely. He'd gone mad for a married woman, and it had all ended in ruin...

Lady Beatrice's voice interrupted her reverie. "It happened the year he turned twenty-one. His father and I insisted he come to London for the Season."

Rose's brows furrowed. She had seen firsthand how dutiful Lord Ashbourne could be, and it seemed odd that he would have resisted such an invitation. "Might he have enjoyed himself too much to leave?" she suggested, recalling his confidence in social situations.

The countess gave a soft laugh. "Quite the opposite! While he was at Oxford, Henry was dreadfully bookish. He preferred his studies to carousing... very unlike his father, I might add."

Rose winced, recalling the day at the Roman ruins when the earl had demonstrated his scholarly expertise. "But you convinced him to go to London?"

Lady Beatrice nodded, her expression growing more somber. "Yes. But it was a disaster.

Rose's head snapped up. "A disaster?"

"His size, my dear," the countess explained. "He's always been so much taller and broader than other men. And when he entered a room, everyone would stare. It made him dreadfully self-conscious."

Rose's heart twisted. She had never thought of him as anything other than confident, almost to the point of arrogance. The idea of him feeling awkward or out of place was hard to reconcile with the man she knew. "It's difficult to imagine him being self-conscious," she said softly

"Now, yes. But back then?" Lady Beatrice shook her head. "It wore on him. He withdrew from society, refused invitations. And just when I thought things couldn't get worse, he met her."

Rose stiffened. "Her?"

"Miss Carla Witherspoon, niece of the Earl of Lindsey," Lady Beatrice spat, her face pinched with remembered fury. "She was the toast of London. Blonde, petite, with the face of an angel. Every eligible man in the city wanted her. Including Henry. He offered for her."

Rose's heart lurched at the thought. "But... she refused?"

"Oh, she did more than refuse," Lady Beatrice said, her voice trembling with anger. "She laughed at him. Called him..." She broke off, visibly shaking. "I can't even say it. Even after all these years."

Rose stared at her. "What did she call him?"

Lady Beatrice's lips tightened, her eyes flashing. "She called him... the Ox from Oxford."

Chapter Ten

"The what?"

"The Ox from Oxford," Lady Beatrice repeated, her tone clipped with indignation. "The little viper called him that after he stumbled and broke a table at Almack's. Not that it was his fault, mind you," she added quickly. "Another man tripped him—claimed it was an accident—but it was poor Henry who took the blame."

Rose's stomach twisted. "That's awful," she murmured, understanding now why the earl's remarks about society women were tinged with bitterness. No wonder he kept the world at arm's length. A thought occurred to her, and she couldn't help but ask, "Whatever became of Miss Witherspoon?"

Lady Beatrice's expression darkened with a haughty sniff. "She married the Marquis of Dumfries," she said, disdain dripping from every word. "He was old enough to be her father, but gold makes up for a great many shortcomings, doesn't it? Now that he's finally popped off, I hear she's hunting for a new title. Rumor has it she might grace the area with her presence this summer. I pray she doesn't. It's going to be difficult enough keeping Henry on board with our plans, but if he hears that woman is nearby..."

"You needn't tell me what that would portend," Rose finished, easily imagining the earl retreating into his brooding solitude. "Still, I wonder if it's better to warn him—forewarned is forearmed, after all."

Lady Beatrice's eyes narrowed. "If Henry even gets a whiff that she's in the vicinity, he'll burrow into this estate like a badger. Promise me you won't breathe a word of it."

Rose hesitated. The last thing she wanted was to defy Lady Beatrice, but deceiving the earl felt wrong. Henry would not appreciate being kept in the dark, and she could only imagine his wrath if he discovered the truth later. But upsetting him unnecessarily seemed equally cruel.

"Very well," she said, giving a reluctant nod. "But if Lady Dumfries does come, I insist his lordship be told. He deserves to know."

The countess opened her mouth to argue, then closed it again with a thoughtful nod. "As you wish, my dear. Now that we've settled that matter, there's something else I've been meaning to discuss."

Rose's curiosity piqued. "What is it, ma'am?"

Lady Beatrice straightened her shoulders, her tone becoming resolute. "I've decided that instead of introducing you as my companion, I shall introduce you as my *guest*. It's more or less the truth, when you think about it. Charlotte did write to say you were welcome here."

Rose winced, remembering her great-aunt's scathing letter from two days prior. If the three-page diatribe was to be believed, the old woman was far from amused by the incident at the inn. She had informed Lady Beatrice that if she wanted "the little hoyden" under her roof, she was welcome to her. But the postscript had stung the most—until Rose learned to act like a proper lady, she wasn't welcome back into the bosom of her family.

"That's very generous of you," Rose said, smiling despite the pang of hurt the memory stirred. "But I don't mind being known as your companion. That's why Lord Ashbourne brought me here, after all."

"You may not care, but *I* do," Lady Beatrice replied with surprising vehemence. "People treat companions and poor relations like they're invisible, and I'll not have you snubbed by anyone in this house. Believe me," she added grimly, "I know the sting of such slights all too well."

Rose raised an eyebrow, intrigued. "Oh?'

Lady Beatrice waved a hand dismissively. "It's an old story, child, and not one worth recounting now. Perhaps someday, when we have more time. For now, I believe I shall retire to my room for a nap."

Rose immediately rose to assist. "Shall I push you to the stairs?"

"If you wish," the countess replied, settling into her chair and covering her legs with the leather apron. "It'll be quicker than calling for the footman."

"I've always wondered why you don't use a wheelchair," Rose mused, guiding the chair through the door with ease. "They're smaller, and you wouldn't need anyone to push you."

Lady Beatrice surprised her by admitting, "I've thought of it. But I didn't want to offend the servants."

"Offend them?" Rose looked down, puzzled. "How would that offend anyone?"

The countess sighed, her voice low. "When I had that ridiculous fall, they fussed so much. They couldn't do enough for me, and if I so much as tried to help myself, they looked devastated." She paused, and Rose could hear the frustration behind her words. "If I had known the entire household would be thrown into such chaos over a silly mistake, I'd never—" She broke off abruptly.

"Never what?"

"Never tried to take that blasted fence." Lady Beatrice laughed lightly, brushing the moment away. "Pride, you see. It got the better of me, and in my case, it came before the fall."

They reached the stairs, where the footman, John, appeared as if summoned. "Ah, there's John!" Lady Beatrice exclaimed, waving him over.

"Will you need anything else, Lady Ashbourne?" Rose asked, stepping back as the stocky footman gently lifted the countess from her chair.

"Heavens, no!" Lady Beatrice smiled warmly. "Just try to relax, my dear. Pray the party doesn't end in disaster—that's all any of us can do."

"If your lordship will kindly refrain from squirming, I shall have this tied in just a moment," Samuels pleaded, swaying on tiptoe as he finessed the final touches of Henry's cravat. "It needs but one more tug, and... there! Perfection!"

Henry stood still, feeling absurdly out of place in all the fuss. He had never enjoyed the formality of it all, the way everyone treated him like a porcelain figure to be polished and perfected. He had always been more at ease in the saddle, away from society's endless demands. Still, Rose would be there, and for some reason, the thought of her seeing him today—seeing him like this—made the entire charade less unbearable.

He turned toward the mirror, bracing himself for disappointment, but blinked in pleasant surprise. The cravat was elegant, the lines clean and crisp. Not as suffocating as the monstrosities he'd worn in his youth. His reflection wasn't quite the 'Ox from Oxford' he dreaded seeing.

His mind wandered, unbidden, to the way Rose had looked at him lately. Not with the disdain he'd expected. Not with mere curiosity.

There had been something else in her eyes, something that tugged at the part of him he had long thought dormant.

"Is everything to your liking, my lord?" Samuels asked, breaking his thoughts.

"It's... fine," Henry muttered, surprised by his own calm. Was he really about to endure an entire afternoon of small talk and pleasantries? The thought of it should have been unbearable. But Rose would be there, he reminded himself again, as if that somehow made it all worthwhile.

"I was concerned about the lapels," the valet continued. "But they do suit your lordship's broad chest far better than wider cuts."

Henry's lips quirked at the compliment, but his thoughts weren't on the lapels. They were back with Rose. She had a way of looking at him that made him feel both exposed and entirely too aware of his own body. He scowled at the mirror, frustrated at his own foolishness. Why did it matter what she thought? She was nothing more than a guest. A distraction, at best. But still, that distraction had gotten under his skin.

"Are you quite certain the gentlemen wear their pantaloons this tight?" he asked, tugging at the fabric clinging to his thighs. The feel of the material reminded him of the way Rose's gaze had lingered on him—whether in exasperation or something more, he couldn't say. But it had been there, hadn't it? That flicker of interest? Or perhaps he was imagining it.

Samuels sighed, as if explaining such things was a chore. "The tighter the fit, the more flattering the silhouette," he said. "You look quite dashing, my lord. The ladies shall swoon."

Henry grunted. "Let's hope not. I'd hate to think all this effort was wasted."

He strode downstairs, his steps heavier than usual as he prepared for the farce of the afternoon. He knew how this would go—empty chatter, polite smiles. All while he tried to pretend he wasn't entirely too aware of one woman in particular.

But when he stepped into the foyer, the house was in chaos.

He found Rose standing near the refreshment tent, her back straight, her hands gesturing with all the confidence of a commanding officer. She was in her element, organizing the chaos with ease. A part of him admired her for it—the way she seemed to navigate even the most demanding tasks without faltering. But it was the way she looked at him, so unflinching, so bold, that truly intrigued him.

"What the devil is going on?" he demanded, though his irritation was more directed at the way she unsettled him than at the change of plans.

"As was the plan, my lord. But it seems the weather has other ideas." Her voice was smooth, calm—teasing, even. She turned to face him, her eyes alight with that spark that always caught him off guard. How was it she never seemed cowed by him? Other women trembled in his presence, but not her

He gritted his teeth. "Shouldn't you wait for the rain to fall before admitting defeat?"

The heavens responded with a flash of lightning and a roll of thunder. Rose didn't gloat, but the gleam in her eye spoke volumes. She crossed her arms, and Henry couldn't help but notice how poised she looked, even in the midst of chaos.

"Harmless clouds?" she echoed, her voice deceptively sweet.

Henry's lips twitched, the tension melting away. "Very well, ma'am. I surrender." He gave her a bow, and despite his best efforts, he couldn't help but admire the way she handled him. No one had ever bested him quite like this. It was both infuriating and intoxicating.

As they walked toward the house, he found his thoughts returning to her again and again. What was it about Rose Sheffield that unsettled him so? Was it the way she never backed down from a challenge? Or was it the fact that, in her presence, he was always acutely aware of the man he was—the man he wanted to be? He wasn't sure, but whatever it was, it had him on edge.

"You're wearing a new jacket," she blurted out, and then immediately blushed. Her candor always caught him off guard, but this—her sudden embarrassment—made him smile. *Ah, so she did notice me.*

"One of my old ones," he said, brushing off the compliment, though he was absurdly pleased by it. "Do you like it?"

The way she looked at him—her eyes full of appreciation—made his chest tighten. "It looks wonderful," she admitted, her voice softening in a way that made him feel... seen. Not as the earl, not as the 'Ox from Oxford,' but as a man.

And that, more than anything, made him want to close the distance between them.

"May I say you look quite dashing as well?" he murmured, his voice lowering. The words slipped out before he could stop them. "That gown suits you."

The flush on her cheeks deepened, and Henry's breath hitched. She was beautiful, and for the first time, he allowed himself to really see her—not as a challenge, not as a thorn in his side, but as a woman. A woman he found far too tempting for his own good.

Before he could say more, she quickened her pace, leaving him to gather his thoughts. But they were already spinning out of control. He was in trouble, he realized, watching her walk ahead of him. Deep trouble.

And for once, Henry Ashbourne didn't mind.

"Oh, look!" Rose interrupted, quickening her pace as she motioned toward the entrance. "Williams is giving us the evil eye. Your guests must be arriving, and we're not there to greet them. He will think me shockingly lax in my duties."

Henry followed her gaze, and a sudden, icy fear gripped him. The cravat that had fit perfectly moments ago now felt like a noose tightening around his throat. His pulse quickened at the thought of enduring an afternoon of forced smiles and simpering introductions. He could almost hear the droning voices, the endless questions about his estate, and worst of all, the thinly veiled attempts by mothers to push their eligible daughters toward him.

Chapter Eleven

Henry felt a strong, sweet urge to mount his horse and ride far, far away

But he swallowed it down, reminding himself that he was an Ashbourne. And Ashbournes did not flee. His father had once stood in the face of cannon fire; Henry could certainly endure a flock of gossiping women. Gritting his teeth, he straightened his shoulders and allowed his hand to tighten, almost involuntarily, on Rose's elbow as if anchoring himself to her before facing the impending storm.

Rose shot him a look, her skin buzzing where his fingers gripped her. There it was again—that undeniable pull, a sensation that sent ripples of awareness through her every time they were close. She shouldn't feel this way, not about someone as insufferably arrogant as Lord Ashbourne, but here they were, walking side by side into the fray.

She inhaled, her senses sharpening with the subtle scent of sandalwood and spice that clung to him, a fragrance as maddeningly intoxicating as the man himself. And he had *looked* at her, really looked at her earlier, when she had complimented his appearance. The memory of that moment, of the way his eyes had softened just for a second, left her unsettled. She had no business thinking of him that way, but her heart betrayed her reason at every turn.

"So you are Miss Sheffield," an elderly woman's voice cut through her musings like a knife, and Rose turned to find herself under the scrutiny of Mrs. Fenswick's pale-blue eyes. The woman looked her up and down, her lips thinning. "Can't say as I've heard of you before. Are you in society?"

"No, Mrs. Fenswick, I am not," Rose replied, managing to keep her tone polite even though she wished the nosy old biddy would move along. She had already been cornered by the squire's mother-in-law for what felt like an eternity, and her patience was hanging by a thread. Another minute of this, and she would be forced to do something drastic, like dousing herself in punch for an excuse to leave.

Mrs. Fenswick sniffed, the sound as condescending as her gaze. "I thought not." She took a noisy sip of punch. "At first, I suspected you might be another of Lady Beatrice's companions, but she assured me you're here as her guest. Curious, I must say. How did you come to meet?"

Rose fought the urge to smirk. She'd like to tell the old bat the truth—how she had met the earl by whacking him over the head with a bed warmer—but she suspected the revelation would send Mrs. Fenswick swooning into a faint, only to revive and gossip her way through the entire county by sundown.

"Her ladyship is an old friend of my great-aunt, the Countess of Waverly," Rose said instead, lifting her chin with an air of superiority. "Perhaps you've heard of her?"

Mrs. Fenswick's jowls quivered, her face flushing a mottled red. "I believe I may have," she muttered, looking away with discomfort.

Rose bit back a smile of triumph. She had spent enough time dealing with society's vipers to know how to handle one. And now, if only she could escape this wretched conversation before the woman recovered.

"I see my neighbor, Mrs. Fashingham, over there," Mrs. Fenswick said, perking up as her gaze landed on a woman dressed in a garish ensemble of purple and gold silk. "If you'll excuse me, Miss Sheffield, I believe I shall go have a word with her."

"Oh, must you leave so soon? How tragic," Rose cooed, unable to resist a little dig.

Mrs. Fenswick gave her a sharp look, but with a mumbled farewell, she waddled away toward her next victim. Rose exhaled in relief, sinking back into her chair with a satisfied smile.

Peace. At last.

Her gaze drifted around the room, taking in the scene. It was all going splendidly, much to her surprise. The rain had started shortly after the last guest arrived, but the decision to move the party indoors had proven wise. The guests mingled happily, chatting and sipping punch, their spirits unaffected by the change of plans. Aside from a few pouting debutantes who had evidently been hoping to show off their new bonnets, everyone seemed content.

Everyone, that was, except for Henry.

Her eyes sought him out instinctively, and there he stood, looking as if he'd rather be anywhere but here. His broad shoulders were stiff, his jaw set in that stern way of his, but beneath the tension, she sensed something else. He was a man out of place, a man who didn't quite fit in the world of tea parties and small talk. But more than that, he was a man who made her heart do ridiculous things, like skip a beat when their eyes met.

As if sensing her gaze, Henry glanced in her direction, their eyes locking across the room. For a moment, the noise and bustle of the party faded into the background. All she could hear was the faint thrum of her pulse, and all she could see was the flicker of something dangerous in his eyes—something that made her stomach flip in a way that had nothing to do with nerves.

What are you doing to me? Rose wondered, her heart tripping over itself.

And then Henry's expression shifted, a flicker of something she couldn't quite place crossing his face before he schooled his features into that familiar, unreadable mask. He broke their gaze and turned back to the group of gentlemen who had been attempting to engage him in conversation.

Rose released a breath she hadn't realized she'd been holding.

What was that? She had expected to feel relief at his retreat, but instead, a strange sense of longing settled over her. It was unsettling, this pull between them, like the shifting tension of a storm building on the horizon. And the more time they spent together, the harder it was to ignore the way he made her feel—like she was teetering on the edge of something she couldn't quite define.

She had always prided herself on being in control, on managing her feelings, her circumstances. But Henry Ashbourne was a complication she hadn't planned for, and the worst part was... she wasn't sure she wanted to resist him.

Across the room, Henry couldn't seem to shake the sensation of Rose's gaze lingering on him. It was like a tether, pulling him in, despite his best efforts to remain detached. Every time he tried to push her out of his mind, she was there—bright, challenging, beautiful. And it was driving him mad.

What was it about her that had him so on edge? She was unlike anyone he had ever known, so sharp-tongued and unflinchingly bold. And yet, beneath that prickly exterior, he had glimpsed something softer, something vulnerable.

Damn it, he cursed inwardly. He had no time for these feelings, and yet... here they were, gnawing at him, making him ache in ways he had long since forgotten.

Rose narrowed her eyes. It was as if the earl were deliberately trying to drive people away. But why on earth would he do that? He could be charming when he wanted to be—she knew that all too well. Their exchanges were often peppered with witty remarks, and his conduct in the drawing room when she measured him for that blasted shirt had bordered on downright flirtation. If he could act like that with her, she reasoned with a decisive nod, then surely he could muster a similar charm for his guests.

Her mind made up, she rose from her seat and strode toward him, determination in every step. His wariness melted away the moment she approached, and the icy veneer in his eyes softened.

"All seems to be going quite well, Miss Sheffield," he said, with a cool nod of acknowledgment. "If there is anything I can do to be of assistance, please let me know.

Rose fought the urge to roll her eyes. Assistance? The man hadn't mingled with a single guest since the party began, yet he had the audacity to ask if he could be of help? Had anyone else made such an offer, she would have accused them of sarcasm. Instead, she took a calming breath, forcing her tone to remain civil despite her growing frustration.

"If your lordship truly wishes to be of service," she replied, a touch too sweetly, "then perhaps you could stop acting like a suit of armor that's strayed from the main hall and start behaving like a host."

His pleasant expression faltered, his features hardening in that familiar, stubborn way. "I do not know what you mean, madam," he said, his voice clipped, fury simmering behind his cool facade. "I have been the perfect host. Did I not greet every guest?"

"Yes, with all the enthusiasm of a man facing his own execution," she shot back, her chin lifting in defiance. "You've avoided every guest since, and the few brave souls who did approach you—well, you sent them running! Is it any wonder they look at you as if you were some ogre?"

His eyes darkened, his posture growing even more rigid. "If you expect me to caper about like some court fool, then you are gravely mistaken."

Rose bit back a smirk, her irritation morphing into something dangerously close to amusement. The image of him prancing about in tight breeches, trying to charm the ladies, was almost too much to bear. But she held her composure, folding her arms and standing firm.

"What I expect, sir," she said, her tone taking on the familiar edge she used when sparring with her father, "is that you do your duty. You can start by speaking to that young lady over there." She nodded toward a modestly dressed young woman sitting alone on the far side of the room.

Henry's jaw tightened, annoyance flashing in his eyes. He glanced over at the delicate blonde, immediately uneasy. "She looks as though she'd faint if a man so much as breathed in her direction," he muttered, remembering his last encounter with a timid young lady.

"Then don't breathe too hard," Rose quipped, giving him a pointed nudge. "Now go. You've dawdled long enough."

With a resigned sigh, Henry straightened and crossed the room, Rose beside him, guiding him as if leading him to his doom. When they reached Miss Felton, the young woman blinked up at them, her large, velvet-brown eyes wide with surprise.

"Good afternoon, Miss Felton," Rose said warmly, offering the young woman a smile. "I believe you've met our host, Lord Ashbourne. I was just telling his lordship that you're from Bath, and he was remarking on the many Roman ruins in the area. Roman antiquities are something of a hobby for his lordship," she added, hoping to spark some life into the conversation.

Miss Felton blinked again, clearly startled. "They are?" she echoed, glancing at Henry shyly. "They are also an interest of mine. We found a Roman statue in our pasture, you know."

Henry's curiosity piqued at once. "Did you now?" His voice warmed slightly as he looked at her. "Which god?"

"We believe it's a representation of the emperor Claudius," Miss Felton said, her quiet demeanor suddenly animated. "The statue wears a crown of olive leaves, which suggests a royal figure, and the face bears a strong resemblance to the images on coins found in the area."

Rose watched with satisfaction as Henry's tension eased, his interest clearly captured. Finally, she thought. If only he could keep this up, perhaps the other guests would see the man she glimpsed behind the scowls and brooding silences

"How long have you been interested in antiquities, Miss Felton?" Rose asked, noting with pleasure that several other guests were casting intrigued glances their way. If she could just keep the earl talking, she was certain others would join in

"Oh, for several years," Miss Felton replied with a soft laugh. "It was my grandfather's passion, and when he passed, he left me his collection."

"I also collect Roman coins and artifacts," Henry said, his tone losing its earlier edge. "Perhaps later I could show them to you, if you'd like."

Before Miss Felton could answer, Rose seized the opportunity. "What a marvelous idea!" she exclaimed. "I'm sure Mr. Paulson would also enjoy seeing them, wouldn't you, sir?" She gestured toward the dark-haired Corinthian who had sauntered over to join them.

"Indeed, I would," Mr. Paulson agreed, giving Henry a teasing look. "Had no idea you were interested in such things, old fellow," he drawled. "To hear Langford tell it, your passions are limited to sheep and oats!"

Henry grumbled, still piqued by Nathanial's absence. "Don't mention that scoundrel to me. The wretch swore he'd be here, only to send his regrets at the last minute."

"His brother summoned him home to Buckinghamshire. Poor Nate had no choice," Mr. Paulson said with a shrug. "Such is the life of the younger son, forever at the beck and call of the heir."

As the conversation continued, more guests gravitated toward the group, and soon the drawing room was abuzz with lively chatter. Satisfied that her work was done for the moment, Rose quietly excused herself, leaving Henry to fend for himself among the crowd.

Once certain the earl was holding his own, she slipped over to Lady Beatrice, who was comfortably settled in a corner of the room, surrounded by a gaggle of matrons. As Rose took a seat beside her, the countess raised her teacup in a mock salute.

"Well done, my dear," Lady Beatrice murmured, her eyes twinkling with approval. "I never thought I'd see the day when my stiff-necked son actually looked as though he were enjoying himself!"

"It took a little encouragement," Rose replied modestly, though she was undeniably pleased. She glanced across the room, where Henry was engaged in a lively discussion. He no longer resembled the cold, aloof figure he'd been earlier, though he still carried that dangerous air that set her pulse racing.

Just as she was starting to relax, she noticed something—a brief flash of discomfort in Henry's expression as Miss Felton spoke to him. His face hardened, and he stepped back, retreating into that cold, impenetrable shell of his. The poor girl looked utterly bewildered before turning and hurrying away, skirts in hand, as if fleeing a dragon.

Rose's satisfaction evaporated. What in the world had he said? She barely managed to maintain her composure as she hurried back toward him, her heart pounding with frustration.

"I leave you alone for fifteen minutes," she muttered, glaring up at him, "and you're back to your old tricks! What did you say to Miss Felton to send her fleeing like that?

His eyes darkened, but he remained as rigid as ever. "I said nothing untoward," he replied through gritted teeth. "She took flight of her own accord."

"Don't be absurd," Rose snapped, her irritation boiling over. "For heaven's sake, will you just—" She stopped mid-sentence, her eyes narrowing. "Wait. Why are you standing like that? You look like a marble statue."

Henry's lips pressed into a thin line. "Because, madam," he said with chilling formality, "I have just split my breeches."

Chapter Twelve

Rose could scarcely believe her ears. Her first instinct was to laugh—how could she not? But one glance at the earl's face, a mask of mortification, told her that would be a terrible mistake. However amusing the situation might seem to her, he was clearly not sharing in her amusement.

"What happened?" she asked, biting her lip, determined to keep her composure.

Henry kept his gaze fixed on the opposite wall, his jaw clenched in that stubborn way of his. "I told that fool of a valet the blasted things were too tight," he muttered, his cheeks darkening to a deep shade of red. "But he insisted it was the height of fashion."

Rose's mouth twitched, her jaw aching from the effort of holding back a smile. "And so it is," she managed to say, though her tone betrayed her struggle. "However, it might be best if we get you out of here and into something… less fashionable."

His gaze snapped to hers, sharp with suspicion. "Are you laughing at me?" he demanded, his outrage simmering just beneath the surface.

"I'm trying very hard not to," Rose replied, unfurling her painted silk fan with practiced ease to hide her grin. "Now hush, and let me think."

She pondered for a moment, racking her brain for a logical, dignified solution to this most undignified predicament. Unfortunately, no grand ideas came to mind. The only memory that surfaced was a rather unfortunate incident from her childhood, involving a tea party, a snake, and her aunt's wrath.

Her sister had invited some neighboring ladies for tea, and Rose, being young and restless, had smuggled a tiny garden snake into her apron pocket. Naturally, the snake escaped at the worst possible moment—right across the toes of the squire's wife. The ensuing chaos was spectacular: women shrieked, skirts flew, and the tea party dissolved into an uproar. Her aunt had vowed never to return, and Rose had spent the rest of the month in her room as punishment.

The thought made her smile despite herself. What if a snake were to get loose in this room? She could almost see it—the women fleeing, the men shouting, and amidst the chaos, Henry slipping out unnoticed to change.

It was, of course, utterly ridiculous. Childish. Impossible. For one, she didn't have a snake. And she could hardly excuse herself to go find one.

"Why are you just standing there like a mooncalf?" Henry growled, his dark brows meeting over the bridge of his nose as he glowered at her. "Do something!"

Rose shot him an annoyed glance. His desperation was palpable, but that didn't excuse his high-handed tone. "I am endeavoring to think of a solution, my lord," she informed him coolly. "But the only idea I've come up with is bound to cause a dreadful scene."

"Possibly not as dreadful as the one I'll cause if I have to leave this corner," he muttered, his expression growing more desperate by the second.

She glanced at him, then at the crowded room, her mind whirring. "If your lordship is certain..."

"So long as it doesn't involve setting fire to the drapes, you may do whatever you please," he snapped, bracing himself as though for battle. "Just be quick about it!"

Rose sighed, resigned to her outrageous plan. "Very well, if that's what you wish."

She swept away from his side and made a beeline for Mrs. Darlington, who was holding court with her daughters, all of them happily oblivious to the earl's predicament. Rose bent down, her voice a conspiratorial whisper as she leaned toward the eldest daughter.

"There's a snake," she murmured.

The girl gasped, her eyes wide with horror. "A snake? In here?"

Rose bit back a laugh at the sight of her horror-stricken face. "A tiny one," she assured her, offering a placating smile. "I think it may have slithered under the settee—"

She didn't even get to finish before the girl leapt to her feet with a scream, knocking the settee back in her haste. Her sisters followed suit, skirts hiked up scandalously high as they fled the room, shrieking like banshees.

Their mother, seeing her daughters in such a state but utterly clueless as to the cause, let out a wail of her own, clasping her hands dramatically to her bosom before swooning—quite artfully—onto the nearest chair. Her performance was so impressive, several other ladies joined in, screams rising into the air as they rushed toward the doors in a flurry of silk and lace.

Within seconds, what had been a perfectly genteel tea party descended into chaos, with women shouting and men scrambling to calm them. A scene, indeed. And one Rose knew would provide delicious gossip for years to come.

She allowed herself a brief moment of satisfaction as she watched the mayhem unfold, before glancing back at Henry. "Now's your chance," she murmured under her breath, meeting his eyes across the room.

For a second, their gazes locked, and despite the absurdity of the situation, there was something electric in the air between them—a silent understanding, an unspoken challenge.

Henry's lips twitched ever so slightly, a glimmer of reluctant appreciation flickering in his eyes. Then, with a curt nod, he slipped from the room, disappearing into the confusion like a shadow.

"I have never been so embarrassed in all my life!" Lady Beatrice moaned some thirty minutes later, her head cradled in her hands as she surveyed the disheveled drawing room. "Really, Rose, how could you?"

"But my lady, as I've already explained!" Rose cried, genuinely wounded by the countess's scathing words. "The situation was desperate, and I had to act! What other choice did I have?"

"A snake?" the countess wailed, throwing her hands up in dramatic despair. "It will be weeks—weeks—before I can lift my head in church again! I shall count myself lucky if any of my neighbors deign to notice me at all. We are ruined!"

Henry, who had been leaning nonchalantly against the mantel, straightened, his expression darkening as he studied his mother. "Come now, Mama, surely you're exaggerating the situation beyond reason," he said coolly. "No one was hurt, and as for anyone daring to snub you—I sincerely doubt it. You are the Countess of Ashbourne. I shall see to it that any who slights you regrets it."

Lady turned her sharp gaze cutting to her son. "As if it's the men I need to worry about!"

"If anyone faces the threat of being snubbed, it's me," Rose said quietly, guilt gnawing at her for causing such tension. She hated being the source of discord, especially between mother and son—it brought back painful memories of quarrels with her own father, and she inwardly flinched at the comparison.

"Nonsense," Henry shot her a stern look, as if daring her to argue. "No one in this household will be snubbed by anyone, least of all you. I shall see to it."

"And how, pray tell, will you manage that?" Lady Beatrice demanded.

"I'll ride into town tomorrow and pay a call on the vicar," he answered decisively, ignoring the astonished look his mother gave him. "And I shall visit the squire and the Darlingtons, just to ensure Mrs. Darlington has recovered from her fit of the vapors."

"You will?" The countess's eyes widened, clearly incredulous. "*Social calls*?"

"I am known to leave the estate on occasion, Mother," Henry replied, a hint of a smirk tugging at his lips as his gaze flicked to Rose. "Despite what some might think, I'm hardly a hermit. I'll ride out after luncheon."

The countess, momentarily speechless, finally nodded. "An excellent plan," she muttered. "But do not go too early. Even in Derbyshire, the Darlingtons keep town hours. And naturally, Miss Sheffield will accompany you."

Rose started in surprise. "Me, my lady?"

"Of course. I cannot go with him," Lady Beatrice said with impatient logic. "And it would be improper for him to call upon unmarried ladies without a female to lend him... respectability. Mabel will accompany you as well. As you are now a guest in our home, we must take every care to protect your reputation."

It all sounded absurd to Rose, but she nodded in deference to the countess's superior knowledge of such matters. "As you wish, Lady Ashbourne." She suddenly felt an overwhelming desire to retreat—her emotions still jangled from the afternoon's events, and the thought of a warm bath and a quiet room seemed wonderfully tempting. Still, she curtsied politely to both the countess and her brooding son. "If you'll excuse me, I believe I shall retire for the evening."

She tried to keep her face impassive as she met Henry's watchful gaze. There was something about the way he looked at her that sent an unsettling thrill down her spine. She swallowed, her voice steady but her pulse quickening. "What time would you like to leave tomorrow, my lord?"

He took so long to answer that Rose nearly repeated the question. "Two o'clock will be fine," he said at last, his voice thoughtful as his eyes lingered on her. "In the meantime, I'll send notes to ensure they expect us. I'd rather not arrive unannounced."

Rose nodded her agreement, then turned to leave, surprised when Henry moved away from the fireplace to join her at the door.

"I'd like a word with you, if you don't mind," he said, his tone low, as he opened the door with one hand and placed the other lightly on her elbow, guiding her out into the hall. His touch was warm, firm, and sent a shiver up her arm.

Once in the hallway, he glanced around to make sure they were alone, and then turned back to her, his gaze intense. "I haven't had the chance to properly thank you for earlier," he began, his voice rougher than usual as he took her hands in his. "I don't know what I would have done without your... creative solution. It was remarkably effective."

Rose's heart skipped a beat as his hands cradled hers, warm and solid. She wasn't naive—this wasn't the first time a gentleman had taken her hand. But the way Henry's fingers curled around hers, the way his touch felt so... intimate, so right—it unnerved her. Her pulse thrummed wildly, and she had to summon every ounce of composure to speak.

"You did say I could do whatever I pleased, so long as I didn't set fire to the drapes," she quipped lightly, though her voice trembled slightly.

The edges of his mouth curved into a wry smile, the kind that made her stomach flutter. "So I did," he murmured, his thumb gently tracing the back of her hand. "Now I wonder if a small fire would have been less dangerous than that imaginary snake. I've never seen a room clear out so quickly."

Despite her conflicting emotions, Rose couldn't help but smile. "It was rather impressive, wasn't it? The vicar was among the first to flee—he practically trampled the young ladies on his way out the door."

Henry's laugh was low, his green eyes bright with amusement. "One would think a man of God would show more courage when faced with a serpent."

As he spoke, his hand slowly moved to her cheek, his fingertips grazing the delicate skin of her jaw before tucking a loose curl behind her ear. The touch was so gentle, so tender, that Rose's breath caught in her throat. Her skin burned where his fingers lingered, and her heart pounded so loudly she was sure he could hear it.

His eyes darkened as he gazed down at her, his focus shifting from her eyes to her lips, lingering there for a beat too long. The air between them crackled with unspoken tension, the space between them charged, alive with something dangerous and heady.

Rose's breath hitched, her body betraying her as she felt a dizzying pull toward him. She could feel the warmth of his body so close to hers, the scent of sandalwood and spice wrapping around her like a spell. Her lips parted, but no sound came—she couldn't think, couldn't breathe.

Without breaking eye contact, Henry raised her hand to his lips, his gaze locked on hers as he pressed a slow, deliberate kiss to her knuckles. The feel of his lips—warm, soft, lingering—sent a shiver of sensation racing through her. Every nerve in her body seemed to come alive, her skin humming with awareness.

"Thank you, Rose," he whispered, his voice rough with emotion as he held her hand against his lips for just a moment longer. "I am in your debt."

Rose's mind was a whirlwind, her thoughts a chaotic swirl of desire, confusion, and something far more dangerous. She knew she should respond, say something, but for the life of her, she couldn't form the words. Her body felt like it was on fire, her heart pounding so hard it ached.

Finally, her pride surged forward, breaking through the haze. She managed a polite smile, though her heart still raced. Tugging her hand free, she stepped back, creating distance between them.

"You are most welcome, my lord," she said, her voice cool and composed, though it felt like a lie. "But now, if you'll excuse me... I am rather tired. Good evening."

Without waiting for a response, she turned and fled, feeling his gaze follow her as she hurried down the hall. Her chest heaved with the effort to breathe, her hand still tingling from the feel of his lips. What had just happened?

As she rounded the corner, she knew one thing for certain: Henry Ashbourne was far more dangerous than she had ever imagined.

Chapter Thirteen

Henry spent the next morning tending to his estate, muscles flexing as he worked, but his mind was far from the task at hand. He couldn't shake the gnawing sensation in his chest, nor the events of the previous evening. His promise to visit the Darlingtons loomed over him like a dark cloud, and he was already regretting the impulse to agree. The thought of being in a drawing room full of gossiping women again was unbearable, yet honor-bound, he couldn't think of a graceful way to back out. He was trapped.

And the worst part was, it was all Rose's fault.

He tossed a bale of hay down from the loft with a grunt, the physical exertion doing little to ease his growing resentment. If she hadn't insisted on parading him around like a proper gentleman, none of this would be happening. He had been perfectly content with the way things were before her arrival, with his isolation and routines. And now, here he was, entangled in social engagements he had no desire for. All because of her.

But even as the unworthy thoughts simmered, a sharp pang of guilt cut through his anger. Deep down, he knew it wasn't Rose's fault. He had let himself be swept along. And if anyone deserved the blame, it was him. He should have known better than to think the 'Ox from Oxford'—as he'd been so scornfully nicknamed—could get through even the simplest of events without making a fool of himself. Perhaps 'ass' would have been a more fitting nickname, he mused bitterly as he hoisted another bale. Although he supposed that lacked the panache of 'Ox.'

"Watch it, now! Mind where you're tossing those bales!" came an indignant shout from below.

Henry glanced down to see McNeil, one of his stable hands, glaring up at him.

"Aye, I'm down here, my lord," the older man continued, his tone tinged with a surprising lack of respect. "Though you're like to flatten me with that last one!"

"My apologies, McNeil," Henry called down, wiping his forehead with his sleeve, his arm streaked with sweat. "I wasn't as attentive as I should've been."

"Maybe we should be tradin' places, then," McNeil grumbled, shaking his head. "A man who can't keep his mind on his work shouldn't be tossing hay bales from the loft."

Henry couldn't argue with that. The truth stung a little, but it was deserved. He had worked hard for the respect of his men, and he wasn't about to jeopardize it by letting his temper get the better of him. With another nod of apology, he went back to work, this time with greater care, though his mind remained elsewhere.

After tossing down the last bale, he descended and began mucking out the stalls, the repetitive, hard labor helping to clear his head. If only life were as simple as mucking out a stall. Dirt, sweat, order—it all made sense here. But society? The intricacies of social graces and whispered gossip baffled him, as did the way Rose had taken to it all, navigating every room with a grace he couldn't help but admire. And, damn it, the way she'd looked at him last night when he kissed her hand...

His pulse quickened at the memory. The softness of her skin beneath his lips. The way her breath had caught, the way she had frozen for just a moment, as if the air between them had sparked with something neither of them could deny. And her curls, those wild, dark strands that always seemed to escape whatever contraption she used to tame them... He'd wanted to touch them, to push one behind her ear, and feel the silken strands slip between his fingers.

"Good morning."

The voice jolted him from his thoughts. He looked up, startled, to find Rose standing in the doorway of the barn, her honeyed eyes wide as they rested on his bare chest. For a second, neither of them moved.

Henry's heart gave a hard thump against his ribs as he set the shovel aside, reaching for the shirt he had discarded earlier. "Good morning, ma'am," he said, pulling the rough fabric over his head, trying to sound as nonchalant as possible, though the sudden flush in Rose's cheeks was not lost on him. "Is there something I can do for you?

Rose swallowed, her gaze lingering on the muscles of his chest, which glistened with sweat. Her throat bobbed, and for a moment, she seemed to struggle to find her voice. "Lady Beatrice... she asked me to fetch you back to the house," she finally stammered, her cheeks growing rosier by the second. "She's worried you'll be late if we don't hurry."

"That's very kind of Mother," Henry replied, grabbing his jacket from the hook by the door. "But unnecessary. I was just about to stop for the day." He could tell by the way Rose's gaze darted to the ground that she was deeply flustered, but he decided not to comment. If he apologized, it would only draw more attention to the fact that she'd seen him half-dressed, and the last thing either of them needed was further embarrassment.

They left the barn in silence, Rose walking stiffly ahead of him, her chin lifted high in an attempt to recover her composure. But the rigid set of her shoulders gave her away. She was clearly unsettled.

After several tense moments, Henry decided to break the silence. He lengthened his stride until he was walking beside her. "And how did you spend your morning?" he asked in what he hoped was a casual tone. "I trust you and Mother have been keeping yourselves busy?"

"Indeed we have," Rose replied, her hands clasped in front of her. She still refused to look at him. "We finished all of the correspondence and went over the menus for the next fortnight."

"Ah. I trust you remembered to tell Cook not to prepare any more oysters?" Henry quipped, determined to set her at ease. "I can't imagine what possessed her to serve them last week. She must know by now that I can't abide shellfish."

"I will have a word with her," Rose muttered, still staring straight ahead.

Henry's patience snapped. He halted abruptly and reached out, gently but firmly catching her by the arm. "Blast it, Rose," he growled, pulling her to a stop. "Will you stop acting so... missish? I'm sorry you saw me without a shirt, but I always take it off when I'm working with the hay. How was I to know you'd be in the stables?"

Her eyes flashed, and she jerked her elbow free, glaring up at him with narrowed eyes. "I am not behaving missishly!" she shot back. "And as for being in the stables, I told you—your mother sent me to fetch you."

"I don't care why you were there," he retorted, his voice tight with frustration. "I'm only saying I didn't mean to shock you."

Rose's lips pressed together in a thin line, and she folded her arms across her chest, her jaw tight. "I wasn't shocked… precisely," she said, her tone softening as she offered him a tentative smile. "Let's just say the less said about the matter, the better."

Henry's jaw clenched, the need to argue rising within him, but he swallowed it down. As a gentleman, he had no choice but to respect her request. "Fine," he said, though he didn't agree. "We'll say no more about it."

They resumed walking, the tension between them still palpable, but Rose was the one to break the silence this time. "I must say, I'm looking forward to seeing more of the countryside today," she remarked, her voice carefully composed. "Is it as lovely as they say?"

Henry's lips twitched in a faint smile, guilt prickling at him. He should have thought to offer her a tour of the area sooner. "Better," he said, feeling a sudden urge to make up for his earlier negligence. "Perhaps, if we have time, I could drive you into Derby to see the Minster," he offered. "It's quite grand—rivals Canterbury Cathedral in my mind."

"Spoken like a true Derbyshireman," Rose teased, and Henry's shoulders relaxed at the sound of her voice. There it was—the playful banter he had grown so accustomed to with her. He didn't like this strain between them. It made him… uneasy.

"And why shouldn't I take pride in my county?" he replied, though his heart sank as they neared the house. Their walk had been too brief, and despite his earlier reluctance, he now found himself wishing they could keep walking. The prospect of spending the afternoon at the Darlingtons no longer seemed so unbearable.

But as he glanced sideways at Rose, her wild dark curls catching the morning light, his thoughts drifted back to the previous evening. He remembered the softness of her hand in his, the way she had looked at him with a mix of surprise and something more—something that had ignited a flame inside him.

Yes, the afternoon could prove quite interesting, indeed.

Rose and Henry, with Mabel in tow, set out for their journey in high spirits. The Darlington estate lay between Thornfield Manor and Derby, and they reached it in less than half an hour. Rose wasn't surprised to find the entire Darlington family assembled in the drawing room, eagerly awaiting their arrival. Mrs. Darlington, it seemed, had fully recovered from her dramatic nerves, and though her greeting to Rose was cordial, it lacked the warmth with which she welcomed the earl.

"Dear Lord Ashbourne!" Mrs. Darlington gushed, thrusting out her hand toward Henry so that he might kiss it. "Such a delight to see you again! And pray, how is your dear mama this morning?"

"She is well, ma'am," Henry replied, a mischievous twinkle in his eye that made Rose fight to suppress a smile. He was clearly doing his best not to laugh at the woman's over-effusive greeting. "I shall be sure to mention that you inquired after her."

"I was going to call on her myself," Mrs. Darlington continued in her overly sweet manner. "So many questions I must ask her. Why, there are parties to plan and clothes to consider! My, but we shall have a gay summer! My girls and I are quite looking forward to it, aren't we, dears?" She gestured toward her daughters, who sat on the opposite settee, perfect blonde curls framing their porcelain faces.

"Yes, Mama," they chorused, fluttering their lashes at Henry in unison, offering him their best dimpled smiles.

"Naturally," Mrs. Darlington sniffed, finally acknowledging Rose, "one hopes the house will be cleared of reptiles before the festivities begin."

Rose, who had begun to grow bored with the tedious conversation, raised an eyebrow at the overt slight. "Oh, there is no need for fear on that account, Mrs. Darlington," she said, a sweet, deceptive smile curving her lips. "I've had a new cage built for Lenny, and I assure you, he won't be escaping again. The poor thing was quite upset by all the excitement. I've been calming him down."

A stunned silence fell over the room as the Darlington family exchanged horrified glances.

"You... have a pet snake?" Mrs. Darlington asked, her voice trembling so much that Rose half-wondered if she was about to swoon dramatically again.

"Just a tiny garden snake," Rose answered, enjoying herself far more than she should. "He's quite colorful. Lord Ashbourne gave him to me," she added, a glint of mischief lighting her eyes as she looped Henry into the outrageous tale. To her delight, Henry picked up the reins at once, his expression entirely serious as he accepted a cup of tea from the visibly shaken Mrs. Darlington.

"I read a fascinating article in one of my farming journals suggesting that snakes are far better than cats at keeping mice at bay," Henry said smoothly, raising his teacup to his lips with elegant ease. "It's worked astonishingly well in the stables, so I decided to try them in the house. We haven't heard a single squeak in weeks."

"Snakes?" Mr. Darlington finally spoke up, his round face thoughtful. "Worth a try, I suppose. Last week, Cook was complaining about vermin in the larder—"

"Edgar!"

"Papa!"

The chorus of horrified feminine voices drowned out the rest of Mr. Darlington's musings. The remainder of the visit was conducted with an air of stiff civility, and by the end, the Darlingtons seemed almost relieved to be rid of their highborn guest and his outrageous companion.

As they set off down the road toward their next stop, Henry couldn't contain his laughter any longer. "You are an absolute menace," he chuckled, handling the ribbons of his light conveyance with obvious pleasure. He had eschewed the more elaborate carriage in favor of something simpler, preferring the freedom to drive himself.

"Snakes in the house," he continued, shaking his head in mock despair. "I can only imagine how quickly that little tale will spread. Soon, the entire neighborhood will be convinced that Thornfield Manor is overrun with vipers."

"Better to be overrun with snakes than to claim mice in the larder," Rose retorted smugly, relishing the havoc she had caused. After so many months of minding her every word, it felt deliciously liberating to be her old, mischievous self again. Perhaps, she mused, she would allow herself an outrageous remark or two each week. She had forgotten how exhilarating it could be.

"That is true," Henry agreed with a grin. "Did you see the look on our hostess's face when her husband let slip about the vermin? I daresay she gave him a thorough scolding the moment we left."

"Oh, I'm sure of it," Rose replied, recalling the knife-like glares Mrs. Darlington had sent toward her hapless husband. "I also noticed that no one dared touch the cakes or sandwiches afterward. Ah, well," she added, batting her lashes in a perfect imitation of the Misses Darlington. "Perhaps the mice will enjoy them."

Their visit to the vicar's home proved far less eventful. Rose was on her best behavior, enduring a long-winded lecture on the sacred

THE BEASTLY EARL AND HIS ROSE 135

duties of a host and hostess, all while choking down a cup of weak tea. Henry, much to his own chagrin, was made to promise he would attend services more regularly. As they left, Rose couldn't resist teasing him about his apparent dereliction of duty toward his immortal soul.

"Never say I've been residing with an atheist," she quipped, laughing as Henry's expression grew mulish. "Shame on you, sir! Have you no regard for propriety?

"I am not an atheist," he protested, tearing his eyes from the road to shoot her an indignant look. "And you, madam, are the last person to talk about propriety. You haven't behaved with an iota of it since the moment we met."

"And you've the nerve to accuse me of telling clinkers?" Rose laughed, too high-spirited to take offense. Turning to Mabel, who had remained quiet through their exchanges, she added playfully, "Mabel, tell this blackguard that I've been the very model of feminine decorum. Have I not?"

Mabel, in her typical blunt fashion, gave a noncommittal shrug. "Wouldn't go so far as to say that," she remarked dryly, "but you haven't tried to dash his brains out again, so I'll give you that."

"There, you see?" Rose turned back to Henry, affecting a prim expression as she folded her hands neatly in her lap. "I've been the very soul of sensibility and moderation. You would do well to follow my example, sir."

Henry let out a low chuckle, his gaze softening as it lingered on her for a moment longer than necessary. "If I followed your example, madam, my reputation would be worse than it already is," he said, though the teasing note in his voice told her that he wasn't entirely bitter.

Rose's heart gave a strange little flutter at the sound of his laughter, and she had to turn away to regain her composure. There was something disarming about the way he had looked at her just now—something that made her pulse race and her thoughts spin in a way they hadn't before. But she quickly buried the sensation, focusing instead on their next stop.

"Now," Henry continued, shaking his head in mock warning, "mind you keep a lock on that outrageous tongue of yours for the rest of the day. I'd rather not scandalize every household in the neighborhood in a single afternoon."

Two days later, Rose sat in her room, going over the last of her lists. The guests had all sent their acceptances, and in less than a week, Thornfield would be overflowing with visitors. The countess had promised that additional staff would be hired, and arrangements were already being made for the finest foods to be brought in from London. Lady Beatrice had left the planning of events entirely to Rose's discretion, a gesture of trust that should have filled her with pride.

Yet instead of satisfaction, Rose felt only a gnawing sense of shame.

The countess was still insistent on secrecy, which meant Lord Ashbourne remained completely unaware of the impending invasion of his home. The weight of the deception pressed on Rose more heavily with each passing day. She hated the idea of breaking her promise to Lady Beatrice, but the thought of continuing to deceive Henry—Henry—weighed on her far more. He had a right to know what was going on under his own roof, and the guilt of keeping such a significant matter from him gnawed at her. She had made up her mind: she would tell him the truth. Even if it meant facing his anger, she couldn't let this charade continue.

With that decision made, the rest of the afternoon passed swiftly. In addition to the usual teas, games of cards, and outdoor strolls, Rose had devised a plan to end the house party with a grand ball. But not

THE BEASTLY EARL AND HIS ROSE 137

just any ball—a costume ball. The idea had come to her in a flash of inspiration, and she had immediately set to work sketching out themes and imagining the splendid costumes. She had never attended a masquerade herself, but the mere thought of it sent a thrill through her. The guests would be delighted, and she was sure it would be the talk of the county for months to come.

However, the matter of costumes was more complicated. She decided to seek the advice of Lady Beatrice, as the older woman would surely have some insights. Rose was so preoccupied with the details of her plan that she barely noticed when she arrived at the countess's chambers, walking in without announcing herself.

"My lady, I was wondering if I might have a word with you," Rose began distractedly, glancing at her sketches. "I've had the most marvelous idea for the ball—

She broke off mid-sentence, her gaze lifting from her notes. Her eyes locked on Lady Beatrice, and the papers slipped from her fingers, fluttering to the floor.

"Lady Ashbourne!" Rose gasped, her voice barely above a whisper. "You can walk!"

Chapter Fourteen

Lady Beatrice turned around, her expression flickering from surprise to resignation as she saw Rose standing in the doorway. "Oh dear," she sighed, setting down the porcelain figure she had been holding, "it appears you have found me out."

"I... I don't understand," Rose murmured, stepping further into the room, her eyes fixed on the impossible sight of the countess standing before the fireplace. "Henry... Lord Ashbourne told me you had been paralyzed in the fall."

"And so I was," Lady Beatrice replied calmly, crossing the room with slow, measured steps to take Rose's hands. "But if you will give me a moment, I promise I will explain everything."

"You can walk," Rose repeated, her voice trembling as she struggled to grasp what she was seeing. Her shock was fading, but in its place, a sense of deep unease began to rise. She remembered Henry's pained expression, the guilt he had carried when he had confided in her about his mother's condition. The realization of how much he had suffered for something that was no longer true made her heart clench.

Lady Beatrice squeezed Rose's hands as if sensing her distress. "It sounds cruel, I know," she admitted, her voice soft but steady. "But I assure you, Rose, I have my reasons. Please, sit with me, and I will tell you everything."

Still reeling, Rose allowed herself to be guided to a seat. Her gaze never left the countess, searching for some explanation—some truth that could make sense of this deception. Lady Beatrice smoothed her skirts and lowered her eyes to her lap, as if gathering the strength to begin.

"When the accident first happened, I truly was paralyzed," she started, her voice quiet but unwavering. "I couldn't move my legs, and the doctors offered us no hope. I was certain I would spend the rest of my life in that blasted chair." She paused, her fingers trembling slightly as they rested in her lap. "Then, slowly, feeling began to return. At first, I didn't dare believe it, but as the weeks passed, it became clear that I was recovering. I cannot tell you how grateful, how relieved I was."

"I can understand that," Rose said gently, reaching out to cover the countess's hand with her own. Her mind raced with thoughts of Henry, and how he had been tormented by his belief that he was responsible for his mother's condition. How could she keep this from him?

Beatrice gave a jerky nod, her eyes lowering. "I... I knew he blamed himself for what happened," she said in a low voice, raising her eyes to meet Rose's. "I was going to tell him that I could walk again, but... Oh, this is going to sound dreadful!"

"What is going to sound dreadful?" Rose asked, her concern deepening as the countess covered her face with her hands.

"I realized that if Henry thought I was still injured, he would be more amenable to getting married," Beatrice confessed, her tone one of a sinner admitting to a terrible crime. She dropped her hands and met Rose's eyes with a pleading look. "You must think I'm terrible, don't you?"

"I don't know what to think," Rose answered, too stunned to be anything but completely honest. She had never heard of such a calculated act in her life. Part of her was horrified by the countess's deception, but another part—however begrudgingly—admired her cunning.

"You do think I'm dreadful," Lady Beatrice sniffed, her green eyes brimming with tears. "And I can't blame you. You're so honest, so forthright. I know you'd never dream of doing anything so conniving."

Rose hesitated, thinking of the times she had used small deceptions to avoid her father's orders. It was nothing of this magnitude, but still... "I wouldn't say that," she muttered, looking away.

"I never intended for the deception to go on this long," Beatrice continued in a small voice. "But weeks turned into months, and the months somehow stretched into a year. I became trapped in that chair by my own lies, just as surely as if I'd been truly paralyzed. I didn't know how to end it. I was at my wit's end until you came."

"Me?" Rose was taken aback. "What do you mean? What has my coming here to do with any of this?"

"For the first time since the accident, that stubborn son of mine agreed to participate in society," the countess explained. "Oh, I know it was just one afternoon," she added quickly when Rose opened her mouth to speak, "and yes, it ended disastrously. But the important thing is that he engaged. Before you, I feared he'd never marry. But when I saw him laughing and talking with Miss Felton... I had hope again."

The memory of Henry's easy conversation with Miss Felton caused a strange pang in Rose's chest, and she shifted uncomfortably in her seat. *Why should that bother me?* She pushed the thought aside, focusing on the matter at hand. "That may be, my lady, but you cannot continue this charade. It's too cruel, especially to him."

Lady Beatrice looked at her with a mixture of desperation and guilt. "I can't just walk up to him and confess everything. He'd never forgive me. It would ruin everything."

Rose sympathized with the countess's fear, imagining how Henry might react to such a revelation. The thought made her stomach tighten. Still, she couldn't allow him to go on blaming himself for something that wasn't his fault.

A lie that lasts this long can only cause more pain. She tapped her foot in thought, trying to think of a way to balance compassion with honesty. Finally, she came to a decision.

"A month," she said firmly, her gaze locking with Lady Beatrice's. "I'll give you a month to reveal the truth, or I will be forced to tell Lord Ashbourne myself."

Lady Beatrice looked as if she wanted to argue, but at the determined expression on Rose's face, she let out a defeated sigh. "Very well," she said, her shoulders slumping. "If you insist."

"I do," Rose replied, her voice steady. The guilt that had been gnawing at her began to ease slightly, though a knot of anxiety remained. "You may start by using a regular wheelchair. It will give you more mobility and help make your recovery appear gradual and believable."

The countess pouted, clearly reluctant. "You mean I'm not allowed a miraculous recovery? What a pity. That would've given our guests something to gossip about for years.

Rose resisted the urge to roll her eyes. "And another thing," she added, ignoring the countess's sarcasm. "I never agreed with your decision to keep his lordship in the dark about our guests. I want your permission to tell him about the party."

"Tell him!" Lady Beatrice gasped, her voice indignant. "But—"

"It's either that or telling him about this," Rose said calmly, folding her arms across her chest and meeting the countess's gaze. "Your choice."

Beatrice's lips pursed in a mutinous pout. "As you wish," she grumbled, clearly unhappy. "But I must say, I'm disappointed in you. I thought you were my friend."

"I am," Rose said steadily, "but I also count myself as your son's friend. And true friends don't deceive each other."

"Don't they?" Lady Beatrice responded with a sly smile. "If you say so, my dear. If you say so."

As Rose left the room, her mind was buzzing with the weight of what had just transpired. How had she been pulled into this deception? And how could she keep the countess's secret for much longer? The thought of Henry, so weighed down by guilt and duty, tugged at her heartstrings, and she felt her resolve tighten.

She would give Lady Beatrice time to tell the truth—but one way or another, Henry had to know.

Chapter Fifteen

After returning to her rooms, Rose found she was too restless to resume her work. The sun streaming through the windows was a sweet temptation, pulling her away from the task at hand. A ride would do her good, she decided, something to clear her mind. She rang for her maid, and thirty minutes later, she was on the mare the earl had selected for her, the warm wind caressing her cheeks as she rode over the rocky rise. She reined in the mare with a joyous laugh, her heart swelling with pleasure as she took in the pastoral scene spread out before her.

The lush green fields stretched before her, neatly enclosed by gray stone fences, while a crystal-clear brook tumbled over moss-covered rocks, its gentle murmurs the perfect accompaniment to her solitude. In the distance, she could see the ruins Henry had shown her on their first ride together, and on an impulse, she decided to ride over for a closer look. She had just started down the steep hill when she heard someone call her name.

Turning her head, she saw Henry riding toward her, his figure silhouetted against the bright sky, his black stallion moving with a fluid grace that stole her breath.

"Good afternoon, Miss Sheffield," he called out, his stallion rearing slightly as he brought it to a halt beside her. "A lovely day, isn't it?"

"Very lovely," Rose replied, her pulse quickening at the sight of him. "I was hard at work in my room when I happened to look out the window and saw all the glorious sunshine. I couldn't remain indoors another moment." If those society ladies could see him now, astride that powerful horse, his hair tousled by the wind, they'd rue their cruel words, she thought with a smile.

His green eyes sparkled at her reply, a teasing light dancing within them. "Deserted your post, have you?" His lips curved into a slow, intimate smile, the kind that sent a warm rush of awareness through her.

Rose's heart gave a telling flutter at the sight of that smile. "So it would seem," she said, unable to resist teasing him in return. "Will you have me shot?"

"That is the usual punishment for desertion," he reminded her, his voice deepening with humor. "But as I've also deserted my post, I suppose I shall have to be lenient."

She fluttered her lashes playfully. "Your lordship is too kind," she murmured, her tone so sweet it made him laugh in response.

As if by silent agreement, they nudged their horses forward, riding side by side in comfortable silence. The warmth of the afternoon, the rhythm of the horses' hooves, and the easy companionship between them created a cocoon of tranquility. Yet, beneath it all, Rose was keenly aware of Henry's presence—of the strength in the lines of his body, the steady confidence with which he held the reins. It made her pulse skitter in ways she refused to acknowledge.

"Where were you headed when I first saw you?" Henry asked after a while, his voice breaking through the quiet. "Anywhere in particular, or were you just letting your horse take you where she would?"

"I was on my way to the Roman ruins," Rose answered, deciding now was as good a time as any to tell him about the impending guests. "I thought our visitors might enjoy seeing it, so I wanted to make sure I could find it on my own."

As expected, he seized on her words immediately. "What visitors?"

"The ones who will be arriving next week," she said, trying to sound nonchalant even as her heart hammered in her chest. "You did say your mother could invite some friends to stay with her, remember?"

"I am well aware of that," he replied, his smile vanishing as his lips pressed into a grim line. "But I had no idea things had progressed so far. How long have you and my mother been planning this?"

"Since the day Lady Amberley's letter arrived," Rose confessed, her throat tightening. Why had her knack for cunning deserted her now, of all times? She used to lie with ease, telling herself it was for the greater good. But now, standing before Henry, her usual defenses crumbled, and the weight of her deception pressed down on her.

"And you never thought to inform me of these plans?" he demanded, pulling his horse to a halt, his green eyes flashing with disbelief. "You and my mother invited guests to my home without so much as a by-your-leave?"

The sharpness of his words lifted Rose's chin. Guilt gnawed at her, yes, but she refused to let him interrogate her as though she were a common criminal. "You already gave your permission, my lord," she reminded him in clipped tones. "And as for keeping you informed, we saw no need to bother you with trifling details—what food to serve, which room to assign. However, if you would prefer, I would be more than happy to turn the entire affair over to you. I'm sure you would do a much better job." She started to turn her horse, fully intending to ride off, but Henry anticipated her move.

In an instant, his hand shot out, gripping her reins, forcing her to stay. The touch of his fingers on hers sent a jolt of awareness through her—hot, electric, undeniable. The tension between them crackled like the air before a storm.

"Rose," he said softly, and the way he said her name—low, dangerous, intimate—made her breath catch. His gaze locked with hers, the intensity in his eyes making her stomach flutter. "I don't care about the food or the rooms. But don't you think, as the master of this estate, I had a right to know about a house full of guests descending upon me?"

His voice was smooth, but the fire simmering just beneath the surface was unmistakable. Rose's pulse quickened, her heart pounding in response to the unspoken heat in his gaze. She should pull away, break the connection, but instead, she found herself leaning in, caught in the magnetic pull between them.

"I... I didn't think..." she stammered, but her words faltered under the weight of his stare. His hand still held hers, and she was acutely aware of the strength in his grip, the heat of his palm against her gloved fingers. It was dizzying, this closeness, and all her logical thoughts scattered like leaves in the wind.

His eyes softened just a fraction, and for a heartbeat, the tension between them shifted, becoming something warmer, something infinitely more dangerous. "Rose," he murmured again, this time softer, his thumb brushing lightly over her knuckles.

Her breath hitched. His touch was so simple, so innocent—and yet it sent a riot of sensation rushing through her body. Her skin burned beneath his hand, her heart raced in her chest, and all she could think about was how dangerously close they were, how easy it would be to close the distance entirely.

But instead of pulling her closer, Henry let go, his jaw tightening as if he were battling some inner war. "Next time," he said, his voice strained, "tell me. I don't enjoy being blindsided."

Rose nodded, unable to form a coherent response. His hand might have released her reins, but the weight of their exchange lingered, heavy and charged with unspoken meaning.

She swallowed hard, trying to compose herself. "I will," she managed, her voice barely a whisper as she turned her horse away, fleeing the tension between them before it consumed her entirely.

For the first time since their unorthodox meeting, Henry no longer seemed like a threat to her well-being, but rather a danger to something much more vulnerable—her heart. And that, she realized with a sinking sensation, was the most unsettling feeling of all.

"You do know," he said, his voice low and smooth, "your temper is regrettably short."

"As is yours, my lord," she shot back, her tone matching his, eyes narrowing slightly.

He regarded her for a long moment, the silence thick between them. Finally, his lips twitched, the ice melting in his jewel-colored eyes. "Perhaps," he admitted at last, "but as I've explained before, I seem to resemble my grandfather—the Beast of Thornfield Manor."

Rose recalled the conversation about the portrait of the formidable fifth Earl of Ashbourne and his fearsome reputation. Her lips curled into a challenging smile. "Then you admit your actions have been beastly?" She dared, praying he would take the words as the jest she intended, and not fly into a temper.

To her relief, a reluctant smile tugged at his mouth. "I should have known better than to cross verbal swords with you," he said, the deep rumble of amusement in his voice making her heart skip. "You've proven yourself a master of the game. Very well then—when may we expect the invading hordes to descend upon us?

His sudden acceptance of the impending guests made Rose blink in surprise. It took her a moment to recover, to find her voice. "They'll begin arriving at the end of next week," she answered, mentally reviewing the preparations. "And the rest will follow the week after."

"The rest?" His brows knitted in displeasure, the idea of his estate overrun by strangers clearly unsettling him. "How many guests are you expecting, precisely?"

"Fifteen," she said as nonchalantly as she could manage. "Not counting the servants and attendants, of course."

"Fifteen?" His frown deepened, and his jaw tightened in clear frustration. "Who, exactly, are these people?"

Rose rattled off the guest list as best she could, watching as Henry's expression darkened with each name. By the time she had finished, his mood had turned decidedly grim.

"I see," he said slowly as they continued to ride, "so that's why she's doing it."

"Why who is doing what?" Rose feigned innocence, but she knew she wouldn't fool him for long.

"Come now, Rose." He laughed softly, the sound low and weary. "It doesn't suit you to play the fool. You know perfectly well that my mother orchestrated this entire house party to throw me together with prospective brides."

Rose tilted her head, considering him. "Well, of course she did! You told me weeks ago that she was anxious to see you wed. What else would you have the poor lady do?"

Her frankness seemed to surprise him. "Allow me to pick my own bride, in my own time?" he suggested dryly, though there was a flicker of something darker beneath the humor in his eyes.

"Don't be ridiculous." She cast him a scornful look. "If men were left to their own devices, the institution of marriage would have expired years ago. You're over thirty, my lord. It's past time you took a wife."

Her words struck a nerve, and Henry's thoughts drifted to the woman he'd once offered his title to—the woman who had rejected not only his title but him. The memory, once sharp and painful, had dulled over the years, but now, he felt something else. Relief. The realization left him uneasy, and in his confusion, he chose to tease Rose instead.

"What about you, Rose?" His voice dipped, deliberately provocative as he used her Christian name to fluster her. "You're in your late twenties, aren't you? Shouldn't you be taking a husband by now?"

"I am but five-and-twenty!" she retorted, her cheeks flushing. "And as for taking a husband, why on earth would I want to do something so harebrained? Husbands are nothing but a bother to an intelligent woman like myself. Even if I were so foolish as to want one, what man would want to leg-shackle himself to a plain-faced, managing bluestocking?"

Her vehement self-deprecation took him aback. "You are not in the least plain," he said, his voice low with a hint of anger. How could she see herself in such insulting terms?

"We're not talking about me," Rose snapped, clearly flustered by her own outburst. "We're talking about you. You're the Earl of Ashbourne, and it's your duty to marry and produce an heir. If your mother must resort to machinations to see you wed, it's only because you've been so behindhand in attending to the matter yourself."

They had reached the ruins. Without a word, Henry dismounted, the tension between them palpable. He moved toward her, his hands reaching for her waist with ease, lifting her down as though she weighed nothing. The heat of his touch lingered as he guided her toward the ruined chapel, and Rose, unsettled by the sudden change in the air, sat on one of the fallen stones. Henry stood before her, resting a booted foot on the stone beside her, his gaze distant as he stared off at the horizon.

"I know I should take a wife," he said, his tone heavy with resignation. "And better than anyone, I know where my duty lies. But knowing what one must do and acting on it are not always the same."

Rose saw the shadows in his expression, the quiet anguish that etched the lines of his face. Her heart ached for him, and she debated whether or not to tell him she knew of his past. After several seconds of internal struggle, she spoke.

"Your mother told me about Lady Dumfries," she said softly, biting her lip when she saw him flinch at the name. "And while it's regrettable that your first love turned out to be a heartless flirt, you mustn't let her memory dictate the rest of your life. There are many other women in the world who would consider it an honor to be your wife."

"Are there?" His lips twisted into a bitter smile. "If such women exist, they've certainly taken their time making their presence known."

Rose's first instinct was to comfort him, but she knew he would view it as pity—an emotion he would undoubtedly abhor. "What can you expect, hiding yourself away here at Thornfield?" she countered, her tone gruff. "Your mother tells me it's been years since you last attended even a simple assembly.

"Did she tell you what happened the last time I attended one of those wretched affairs?" His voice tightened with suppressed emotion.

"I asked two ladies to stand up with me for a quadrille. Two. And they both fainted."

Rose thought of how imposing Henry could be, especially with that stern expression of his, but that hardly excused the fainting fits of those silly chits. "Well then," she said, her tone light with teasing, "all I can say is that you obviously asked the wrong ladies. Can you imagine either Miss Felton or myself behaving in such a singularly foolish manner?"

His posture stiffened, and he straightened to his full height, eyes dark and unreadable as they locked onto hers. His voice was low, challenging. "Are you saying you would dance with me?" His gaze held her, steady and unyielding, as if daring her to deny it.

The unexpected question threw her. For a heartbeat, she considered laughing it off, but something in his expression, in the intensity of his focus, stopped her cold. She swallowed, nerves fluttering unexpectedly. "Of course, I would," she said, though a nervous laugh escaped her. Her mind wandered to the years she'd spent in Richmond, sitting with the dowagers, watching the dancers longingly while pretending not to care.

"Alright then."

"Alright?" She blinked in confusion. "Alright what?"

"Alright," he repeated, his calm voice doing nothing to hide the quiet demand beneath. "I will attend the next assembly, but only on one condition—you must be there, and you must dance with me."

Her breath caught, her stomach doing a strange, excited flip. The sheer audacity of his request stunned her into silence. Had it not been for the seriousness in his gaze, she might have laughed out loud. Instead, she found herself caught between disbelief and nervous tension. "My lord," she began, voice faltering as her nerves betrayed her, "I am your mother's companion—"

"No, you're not," he interjected smoothly, stepping closer. His voice, low and commanding, left little room for argument. "You are a guest here, Rose, and no one will think it odd if I ask you to dance. Quite the opposite, in fact. What kind of host would I be if I didn't stand up with you?"

Her breath hitched at the way he said her name, soft and possessive, as though her title had vanished into thin air. His logic was sound, and she knew all too well that there would be more scandal if he were to slight her at the assembly than if he danced with her. Still, something in her balked at the idea.

"Yes, I suppose there is that," she managed, her voice a little breathless. "But I would still prefer you ask one of the other ladies. Miss Felton, perhaps, or one of the Misses Darlington. And, of course, once your mother's guests arrive, you will have any number of women to choose from as partners." Her voice trailed off as a sudden thought struck her, and she turned her gaze back to him, suspicion creeping into her eyes. "Wait a moment... Do you dance, my lord?"

His jaw clenched, and she noticed the faintest tightening of his fists at his sides. "Yes, I dance."

She wasn't quite ready to let him off the hook just yet. "What about waltzing?" she pressed, her voice laced with mischief.

He frowned, clearly puzzled by her line of questioning. "What of it?"

She gave an exaggerated sigh, folding her arms across her chest as if addressing an obstinate child. "Do you waltz?"

His frown deepened. "It wasn't the fashion when I was in London," he admitted stiffly. "I'm afraid I do not. But I doubt it will be an issue at the assembly. Derby is not London, and such scandalous behavior is frowned upon here. I'd be surprised if the master of ceremonies allows a single waltz, if that.

"Perhaps," Rose said, a thoughtful look crossing her face as she recalled the outcry the first time the waltz had been performed in Richmond. "But your mother's guests will be rather more cosmopolitan, I suspect. They'll expect the waltz to be played at the costume ball."

Henry opened his mouth to ask what costume ball, but the question died on his lips as a far more delightful scheme came to mind. A slow, wicked smile curled his lips, and he crossed his arms, leaning in just enough for his voice to drop to a velvety pitch. "I see no great difficulty," he said, each word a sensual promise. "If you wish me to waltz, then you'll simply have to teach me."

The riot of color that flooded Rose's cheeks was a sight that delighted him to no end. "I can't teach you to waltz!" she protested, flustered, her hand flying up to her throat.

"Why not?" His grin widened, his amusement unmistakable. "Are you saying you don't waltz?"

"Of course, I do!" she spluttered, her heart thudding in her chest. "That is to say, I've learned the dance... but I've never actually performed it."

He gave her a satisfied nod, as if that settled the matter. "Then we'll learn together." His gaze never wavered from hers, the intensity of it making her stomach flip once more. "When would you like to start?

Her mouth opened to protest further, but as the realization of her defeat sank in, she could only gape at him in helpless frustration. He had outmaneuvered her entirely. "You're enjoying this, aren't you?" she muttered, glaring up at him, her tone laced with reluctant admiration.

His grin turned devilish. "Not yet, my dear," he said, his voice dropping to a low, teasing purr. "But I will."

Chapter Sixteen

Over the next few days, Rose found herself in a whirlwind of activity, rushing about Thornfield to ensure everything was in readiness for the guests' arrival. The rooms were cleaned, fresh linens laid, and the last of the entertainment plans were falling into place. Picnics, excursions into Derby to see the famous minister, and, of course, countless card games and dancing parties were arranged to keep their visitors amused. Rose was determined that not one of them would have the chance to grow bored.

After much discussion with the countess, they had decided on a costume ball—a rare treat these days, as Lady Beatrice had pointed out. Its novelty would make it the talk of the neighborhood for months. Invitations had been dispatched advising the guests of the need for costumes, and one of the footmen had been sent to Derby to ensure there would be plenty of costumes available for those who hadn't brought their own.

The day before the first guests were set to arrive, Rose was in the cellar, completing one last inventory. She and the butler had marked out several bottles of port and brandy for the occasion, but Rose wanted to be certain there would also be lighter wines and sherry on hand for the ladies. She was examining a bottle of Spanish sherry when she heard footsteps and Henry's voice calling her name.

She looked up, and a moment later, he came clattering down the steps, his expression both impatient and amused.

"There you are," he said, his hands planted firmly on his hips as he regarded her. "What in the devil are you doing down here? I've been searching for you everywhere."

Rose handed the bottle to the silent butler and dusted her hands. "William and I are making sure the cellar is adequately stocked." She raised a brow at Henry's sudden appearance. "Is something amiss?"

She prayed he hadn't come to ask about his mother's mysterious lack of recovery. So far, Lady Beatrice had shown no inclination to begin her "miraculous improvement," and Rose was beginning to wonder if the countess would call her bluff.

"Never mind that now." Henry ignored her question entirely and, before she could object, reached out to grab her hand. "I want you to come with me."

Taken by surprise, Rose allowed herself to be led up the stairs, her skirts gathered in one hand as she tried to keep pace with his long strides. "Where are we going?

"To the ballroom," he tossed over his shoulder, his tone maddeningly cryptic. "There's something I want to show you."

Her mind immediately jumped to the chandelier. *Oh, heavens*, she thought miserably. She hadn't had time to get the thing cleaned yet. But it wasn't the chandelier that awaited her. Instead, when they entered the ballroom, Rose's gaze landed on a small, bespectacled woman seated at the pianoforte.

"This," Henry announced with a sly grin, "is Miss Brickley. She teaches music at one of the local ladies' seminaries, and she has kindly agreed to play for us." He paused, turning to Miss Brickley with a warm smile that had the old woman blushing like a debutante. "Haven't you, Miss Brickley?"

"Oh yes, my lord," she stammered, clearly flustered. "I'll be delighted to assist."

"Good." Henry turned back to Rose, his grin widening, his eyes gleaming with mischief. "Now, as I've mentioned, I've never actually performed the waltz. But I'm not such a savage that I'm completely unfamiliar with it." Without warning, he slipped an arm around her waist, pulling her firmly against him. "Is this correct?"

Rose's cheeks flamed at the feel of his strong chest pressed against her. "I... yes, my lord," she managed to stammer, "though perhaps not quite so tightly."

"Is that better?" he asked, loosening his grip ever so slightly.

She took a step back, relieved to have a bit more space between them. "Yes, my lord."

If he noticed the breathless quality to her voice, he was too much of a gentleman to comment. Instead, he took her right hand in his, his fingers curling around hers with an intimacy that made her pulse race. "And if I recall correctly," he murmured, his breath stirring the hair on the top of her head, "I am to hold your hand like this?"

Rose tried to ignore the fluttering sensation in her chest, telling herself firmly that he was only trying to unnerve her—and that she would not give him the satisfaction of knowing he was succeeding. Taking a deep breath to steady herself, she turned to Miss Brickley, who was watching them with unconcealed interest. "If you would start playing, Miss Brickley, we'll begin."

Turning back to Henry, she kept her voice steady. "Listen to the music," she instructed, her gaze fixed on a safe point somewhere just beyond his shoulder. "If you've ever danced a minuet, you'll recognize the cadence. Can you hear it?"

He listened intently, his eyes narrowing slightly as the melody filled the room. "I believe so," he replied. "My tutors always claimed I was musically inclined. I should be able to whirl you about the floor without disgracing us both."

Rose ignored the teasing note in his voice and focused on the front of his shirt. "The important thing to remember," she continued, "is that your partner will be looking to you for guidance. She'll follow your lead, and it's essential that you learn to signal your intentions without speaking."

"And how do I do that?" he asked, his tone making it clear that he found the entire thing amusing.

Grinding her teeth in frustration, Rose wished—not for the first time—that they weren't in the presence of a third party. If Miss Brickley weren't watching so avidly, she would've found some way to make him pay for his insolence. Instead, she forced herself to smile sweetly.

"You give her a slight squeeze, my lord," she replied, her fingers digging into his shoulder with more force than necessary. "Like this."

If she was hoping to make him flinch, she was disappointed. He didn't even blink, though the mischievous gleam in his eye grew more pronounced. "Let me make sure I've understood you correctly, ma'am. When I wish my partner to turn, I do... this?" His hand slid forward, his grip tightening just enough to remind her of his strength.

Rose's breath hitched, but she refused to give him the satisfaction of knowing he had rattled her. "Yes," she ground out, glaring up at him as she conceded temporary defeat. "That is correct, my lord. Shall we begin? One, two, three... one, two, three..."

To her surprise, Henry proved to be an excellent student. After a few stumbles, he caught the rhythm and began guiding her effortlessly across the ballroom floor. By the third turn, Rose found herself laughing in spite of herself, the earlier tension forgotten in the sheer enjoyment of the moment.

"Well done, sir!" she exclaimed, her eyes sparkling as she smiled up at him. "And here I thought you said you didn't waltz.

"I didn't think I did," he replied, his lips curving into a smile that sent her heart skittering. For a moment, time seemed to slow. She was acutely aware of the warmth of his breath on her skin, the steady beat of his heart against her own. His eyes, a deep emerald, held hers with an intensity that made her pulse quicken.

Her fingers tightened on his shoulder, and for a brief, dizzying moment, she forgot where they were. Henry's head dipped toward hers, his gaze darkening with something she wasn't sure she was ready to name.

"There you are!" A voice shattered the fragile moment, and they sprang apart as Lady Beatrice wheeled herself into the room in a brand-new chair.

Henry recovered first, though Rose could still feel the heat of his gaze lingering on her. He turned to his mother, his tone a mixture of concern and irritation. "What are you doing in that contraption?" he demanded. "Where's your other chair?"

Lady Beatrice waved him off with a dismissive gesture. "That monstrosity? It's where it belongs. Those things"—she patted the armrests of her new chair—"are for old ladies. Do you think I want our guests to think I'm one foot in the grave?"

"Certainly not, but—"

"Good," she interrupted, her tone brooking no argument. She turned to Rose with a smile. "There you are, my dear. Lady Amberley will be arriving shortly, and you asked me to remind you that you wanted to change into something more suitable."

Rose had made no such request, but she was grateful for the excuse to leave. "Thank you, my lady. I'll go and change at once." She turned to Henry, forcing herself to meet his gaze. "Will you be joining us, sir?

Henry's eyes remained unreadable, though his jaw tightened as he studied her face. "I wouldn't dream of missing it," he replied, his voice rough with barely restrained emotion.

Rose gave a jerky nod, then turned and fled the ballroom, her heart pounding as if all the hounds of hell were on her heels.

Chapter Seventeen

Lord and Lady Langwick, accompanied by their daughter Lady Margaret, were among the first guests to arrive. The marchioness and the countess were old friends, and they greeted each other like long-lost sisters. The two ladies quickly retreated to the far corner of the drawing room to renew their acquaintance. Since Henry had been called away on an emergency, it fell to Rose to entertain the marquis and his beautiful daughter.

Lord Langwick accepted the earl's absence with a mutter and a shrug, but Lady Margaret was far more vocal in her displeasure.

"I must say, I am quite disappointed," Margaret sighed, her Cupid's-bow mouth set in a pretty pout as she accepted the glass of lemonade Rose handed her. "I have heard so much about his lordship, and I was really looking forward to meeting him."

"Lord Ashbourne should be home shortly," Rose said politely, though she couldn't quite understand what it was about the lively brunette that set her on edge. "One of the tenants was trampled by a horse, and he's gone to check on him."

Lady Margaret, seemingly uninterested in the explanation, continued with her chatter. "All of my friends are positively beside themselves with envy. He hasn't been in town for ages, and there are the most delicious stories circulating about him."

She leaned in slightly, her eyes bright with mischief. "Tell me, Miss Sheffield, is the earl really as savage as they say he is?"

Rose's fingers tightened around her glass, and for a moment, she was sorely tempted to spill its contents down the front of Lady Margaret's lovely gown. "Lord Ashbourne is not the least bit savage," she replied, setting the lemonade down with more force than necessary. "He may not be a town fop, but he is hardly a barbarian. In fact"—Rose fixed Margaret with a sharp look—"he is an excellent dancer. I have never waltzed with a man half as graceful."

Margaret blinked, clearly taken aback. "But how can that be?" she asked in the tone of a child discovering there is no Father Christmas. "One hears—"

"One hears many foolish things," Rose interrupted, her patience wearing thin. "That doesn't mean one must believe them. His lordship is your host, Lady Margaret, and I'm sure you are far too much of a lady to indulge in idle gossip about him."

Margaret's cheeks turned as pink as her ruffled muslin gown, and she set her glass down with a petulant bang. "If you would be so kind as to have one of the servants show me to my room," she sniffed, her tone as cold as she could muster, "I believe I shall retire. I've the most dreadful headache."

Rose rang for the maid with the same air of forced politeness, but the moment Margaret had flounced out of the room, another carriage arrived at the front of the house. Soon, Rose found herself once again entertaining a group of giggling, wide-eyed debutantes. By the time she had escorted the last of them to their rooms, all firmly put in their place, her patience was beginning to fray at the edges.

"My word, Lady Ashbourne," she sighed the moment she was alone with the countess, "what on earth did you write in those letters? They seem to look upon your son as if he were an exhibit in the Royal Menagerie."

Lady Beatrice's lips twitched with amusement. "Well, my dear, Henry has only himself to blame." She leaned back in her new wheelchair, clearly pleased with herself. "He's the one who chose to turn his back on society, so we can't fault them for forming their own opinions. Besides, young ladies do enjoy a bit of mystery in a man. It makes them seem far more dashing than they really are."

"One step removed from a cage, more like," Rose muttered, recalling the way one young lady—Miss Ann Deveau—had shivered in horrified delight at the thought of meeting the Black Earl.

"Nonsense, child," Lady Beatrice replied breezily. "You pay too much mind to society's idle chatter. If these chits were yawning at the mention of Henry's name, then we'd have cause for concern. As it is..." She gave a delicate shrug.

Rose bit her tongue but resolved to have a quiet word with Henry before things got out of hand. If these young women started fainting or acting as though they expected to be ravished the moment they met him, she doubted she'd ever convince him to venture into society again. He would undoubtedly retreat into one of his brooding silences, and the entire house party would be a disaster.

The thought crossed her mind that such an outcome might be to her advantage, but she ruthlessly pushed it aside. The purpose of this gathering was to help Henry reestablish himself in society, and she was determined to see it through. The only difficulty would be convincing him not to lose his temper the first time one of these young women called him "the Black Earl" to his face.

But how? The question occupied her mind as she braced herself for the next wave of visitors.

His shoulders were slumped with weariness as Henry made his way down the back hallway from the kitchens. It had been a hellish day, and he longed for the privacy of his room and a few hours of blessed silence. Unfortunately, with the house teeming with guests, such luxury would have to wait. Just as he was cursing his lack of solitude, a door opened ahead, and a woman stepped out, nearly colliding with him. He opened his mouth to offer an automatic apology, only to realize it was Rose.

"Have a care, madam," he teased, reaching out instinctively to steady her. "This is a racetrack, you know."

"Henry! I mean... Lord Ashbourne!" she exclaimed, but the sound of his name on her lips pleased him more than he cared to admit.

"And it's a good thing for you too," he continued, making no effort to step aside and let her pass. "If I had been one of our guests, you might have sent me tumbling. For once, it seems my size has its advantages."

She smiled faintly, but instead of responding with her usual sharp retort, she placed a hand on his arm. "Is everything all right?" Her misty eyes searched his face with concern. "How is the man who was injured?"

Rather than shelter her from the grim reality, Henry answered honestly, knowing she would appreciate the truth. "Thankfully, he'll recover, but it will be months before he can walk again." He sighed, feeling some of the tension leave his body at the comforting warmth of her touch. The morning had been brutal, spent holding the man down while his shattered leg was set. The memory of the man's agonizing groans still echoed in his mind. He pushed the grisly scene away and allowed himself to take in Rose's appearance.

She had set aside her usual plain attire some weeks ago, but this was the first time he'd seen her dressed so fashionably. The yellow striped muslin gown suited her, and he found it entirely enchanting. "How is everything here? Have the guests arrived?" His gaze lingered on a loose tendril of hair that had escaped from her chignon, and he resisted the impulse to tuck it back into place.

As if suddenly aware of the proprieties, Rose withdrew her hand from his arm, stepping back quickly. "I'm glad you mentioned the guests. I feel I ought to warn you."

"Warn me?" He raised an eyebrow, confused. "What on earth are you talking about?"

She hesitated for so long he wondered if she'd decided not to answer. Just as he was about to press for an explanation, she gave a nervous laugh. "It seems the clergy was right, my lord—reading Byron does have a most lamentable effect on the female mind."

Henry's eyes narrowed in suspicion. "Meaning?"

"Meaning," she said lightly, though he could hear the teasing note beneath, "that you, sir, have been cast in the minds of our younger guests as the very epitome of one of Byron's brooding heroes."

"What?"

She laughed, still avoiding his gaze. "You must know the ladies regard you as a dark, mysterious lord. To them, you're the stuff of legend, and they are completely in awe of you. I thought you might like to know."

Henry felt heat rise to his cheeks. He dreaded being stared at as if he were some sort of oddity, but the last thing he'd expected was to be seen as a romantic figure. The thought was so absurd that a reluctant smile tugged at the corners of his mouth.

"Byron?" he repeated, his lips twitching as he looked down at her.

"Undoubtedly. His lordship's epic poems are all the rage among young ladies these days," she said, raising her eyes to meet his. "If you want my opinion, they're already half in love with you. Your mother tells me there's nothing like a dark and mysterious reputation to make a lady go weak at the knees. We may need to send for an entire case of smelling salts if you plan on surviving the next fortnight."

Henry chuckled at the image, his spirits lifting for the first time all day. Suddenly, the prospect of Thornfield being overrun with guests didn't seem so grim. He hadn't even realized they had begun walking down the hallway together, his hand resting lightly on her arm as they made their way back to the front of the house.

In honor of the guests' first night at Thornfield, several members of the local gentry had been invited to dinner. Rose was relieved to see that Miss Felton had accepted her invitation. The young woman looked lovely in a modest gown of topaz satin, her long curls gathered back. She approached Rose with a grateful smile.

"Miss Sheffield," Miss Felton greeted her, casting a wistful glance toward Lady Margaret, who was dressed in a stunning gown of white silk festooned with pink rosebuds. "I fear I may be a trifle underdressed."

Rose followed her gaze, noting how the lively brunette, Lady Margaret, flirted shamelessly with Henry. He, to Rose's dismay, seemed to be holding up admirably under the young lady's attentions.

"She is young yet, so we must forgive her excesses," Rose replied in a low tone, so their conversation wouldn't be overheard. "I am only surprised her mama allowed her to wear something so... extravagant."

Miss Felton's gaze flicked to the Marchioness, who was seated to Henry's left. "I'm not," she muttered, then quickly covered her mouth, her eyes widening in horror. "I cannot believe I said that. How awful of me!" Her cheeks flushed with embarrassment.

"Psh," Rose replied gruffly, feeling like a blackhearted sinner for corrupting Miss Felton's gentle nature. "If you had heard the way she and her daughter were dishing up gossip earlier, you wouldn't feel so guilty. Besides," she added, casting a glance at Lady Margaret's elaborate gown, "it's not less than the truth."

"What are you two whispering about?" Lady Beatrice's voice broke into their conversation, her expression alight with curiosity. "You've been sitting with your heads together all evening.

"We were discussing Roman ruins, my lady," Rose lied easily, barely missing a beat. "Miss Felton was just telling me there are several in the area that might interest our guests."

"You must be referring to the base of the minister and the old tower," Nathan Langford, seated nearby, added smoothly, offering an encouraging smile to both ladies. "They're said to be part of the Principia."

"Principia?" Rose asked, grateful for the timely intervention. She had met Mr. Langford earlier that evening and found him quite charming. Despite his polished appearance, he was remarkably approachable, and she understood why Henry was fond of him.

"The Garrison headquarters," he explained. "Derby was once the military capital of Roman Britain."

His hazel eyes rested briefly on Miss Felton, who smiled demurely. "I had no idea you were interested in Roman history, Miss Felton."

"There is much about me, sir, that you do not know," Miss Felton returned with a quiet, almost teasing smile. "But yes, it is one of my interests. I believe it's a subject of interest to you as well, my lord?" She turned slightly, directing her question to Henry, who had moved to stand beside Langford.

"As a matter of fact, it is," Henry replied with a smile.

"Perhaps we might all ride into town tomorrow and visit these ruins," Lady Langwick suggested, her voice carrying an edge of disapproval as she glanced at her daughter, clearly annoyed that Margaret was allowing another young lady to attract so much masculine attention. "My daughter is equally fond of ruins, aren't you, dearest?"

Margaret, quick to respond to her mother's subtle prompting, put on a bright smile. "Oh yes, I just adore them."

"Are they haunted?" Miss Dorth called from her place halfway down the table, her voice eager. "I do love a good ruin! One of my favorite novels was set in a crumbling chapel haunted by the most dreadful spirit. I declare, I could scarcely finish it!"

Henry chuckled at the idea, shaking his head. "As for spirits, ma'am, I cannot say. But the ruins are quite spectacular. If everyone is agreeable, I'm sure we can arrange something."

The proposed excursion became the main topic of conversation for the remainder of the meal, and by the time the ladies rose to leave the gentlemen to their port, everyone was in an unexpectedly cordial mood. The ladies retired to the drawing room for gossip, and when the gentlemen finally joined them, it was clear that the day's travels had taken their toll on the guests. It was decided there would be no card-playing that night, and the party soon broke up.

Miss Felton and her cousin, who acted as her chaperone, also prepared to leave. A small battle of wills ensued when Mr. Langford insisted on escorting them.

"You are very kind, sir," Miss Felton said stiffly, her voice betraying the cool politeness of her words, "but it is unnecessary, I assure you. Mrs. Thorne and I managed to drive here without being attacked, and one can only assume we shall be able to make the return trip just as safely."

"Perhaps I am the one in need of protection from you," Mr. Langford replied with a grin, his eyes glinting with lazy provocation. "Besides, as we are both traveling the same road, it only makes sense that we go together. Unless, of course, you object to my company?" He raised a mocking eyebrow.

Faced with the direct challenge, there was little Miss Felton could do but acquiesce. After bidding their host and Rose a polite, if somewhat stiff, goodnight, she departed in a flurry of satin skirts. Rose watched her go, perplexed by the usually well-mannered young woman's behavior. However, with the squire and the Darlington family also taking their leave, there was no time to linger on the matter.

Once alone, Lady Beatrice collapsed against her chair with a sigh of relief.

"Thank heavens that's over." Lady Beatrice fanned herself vigorously. "I cannot think what possessed me to invite so many people here, and this is only half of them!"

"Are you all right, Mother?" Henry asked, his eyes narrowing with concern as he studied her closely.

"Of course I am!" she replied, drawing herself up with a touch of indignation. "I am not so aged that a simple dinner party will send me to my grave! Now, are you truly planning to go to Derby tomorrow, or was that all talk to appease the ladies?"

He looked as though he were suppressing a laugh. "I had intended to make a trip to Derby, although not necessarily tomorrow."

"And why not tomorrow?"

"Wasn't it that impertinent Franklin fellow who said, 'Never leave until tomorrow what you can do today'? If it's good enough for an American, surely it's good enough for you."

Henry chuckled and accepted his defeat with a good-natured bow. "As you say, Mother. I will see what I can do."

"Good." She turned to Rose, a mischievous gleam in her eyes. "And will you be going with them?"

"I thought I might," Rose replied, her smile widening at the sight of Henry being so easily managed by his mother. "But if I am needed here—"

"Nonsense!" Lady Beatrice interrupted before she could finish. "That is precisely why you must go. You've been working like a Trojan this past week, and a bit of exercise is just the thing to put some color back in your cheeks. Besides," she added with a sly glance, "you can set a good example for the younger ladies."

"Miss Sheffield is our guest, Mother," Henry interjected in a slightly reproving tone. "It hardly seems proper to expect her to sing for her supper. I'm sure Lady Langwick and the other mamas will provide adequate supervision."

Lady Beatrice raised her gaze heavenward in exaggerated exasperation. "As you wish, my dear. I'm certain you know best."

They had spent the next hour chatting idly, with Lady Beatrice keeping them both entertained as she ruthlessly dissected the evening's guests and their numerous follies. Even Henry joined in, his dry, weary observations sending Rose into fits of delighted laughter.

But as the evening wore on and Lady Beatrice excused herself, the conversation between Rose and Henry grew quieter, more intimate. Time seemed to slip away unnoticed. Rose only began to sense its passage when Henry startled her by leaning forward, capturing her hand in his. The warmth of his touch was electric, and she felt a sudden, unfamiliar heat bloom in her chest.

"I wish you would do me the honor of addressing me by my Christian name," he said, his voice deep and serious as his eyes met hers. The weight of his gaze held her captive. "We have long since passed the need for such stiff formalities."

Rose's heart leapt at his words, her pulse quickening at the feel of his hands cradling hers. "I... I would like that," she murmured, feeling the soft burn of his name on her lips. "Henry." The sound of it felt strange but thrilling. "And I give you leave to use my given name as well... if you wish."

His lips curled into a slow, intimate smile. "I wish," he said softly, giving her hand a gentle squeeze before leaning back in his chair, though his eyes never left her face. "Now that we are on such intimate terms," he continued, his tone lighter, "perhaps you'll tell me what you and Miss Felton were really discussing at dinner."

Rose blinked, caught off guard. "I beg your pardon?"

"Don't try to feed me that nonsense about Roman ruins and Derby." His smile widened as he saw her incredulous look. "I saw your face, Rose. You weren't discussing anything as mundane as antiquities."

Rose was taken aback by how well he had read her. He was sharper than she had given him credit for, and the realization both unsettled and intrigued her. She shot him a playful but resentful look from beneath her lashes.

"Actually, my lord"—she deliberately emphasized his title, letting him know she wasn't quite ready to let down her guard—"we were discussing something even more prosaic than antiquities."

He raised a brow. "And what might that have been?"

"Fashion," she replied with a half-truth, her tone sweet but edged. "Miss Felton was afraid her gown was inadequate for the occasion, and I was reassuring her. Does that satisfy your curiosity, Henry?"

He held her gaze, a smirk tugging at his lips. "For the moment," he conceded, though his thoughts were far from settled. He wondered what she would do if he kissed that defiant pout right off her lips. The thought had been plaguing him for days now, and suddenly, he knew he couldn't go another moment without discovering the answer for himself.

Setting aside every scrap of caution he had carefully cultivated over the years, Henry leaned forward. His hands closed around hers, drawing her closer as he rose to his feet, gently but inexorably pulling her up with him.

"Henry!" Rose's hands flew to his broad shoulders, her eyes wide with surprise. "What are you doing?"

"What do you think I'm doing?" His voice was low, amused, but his green eyes had darkened with an intensity that made her pulse stutter. "Rose, you cannot be that innocent."

She stared up at him, a storm of emotions churning inside her. His arms were around her now, firm and possessive, and her heart raced—not with fear, but with something far more dangerous. Surely it couldn't be desire? Her knees felt weak, and her confusion only deepened as she pressed a hand against his chest in a futile attempt to push him away.

"If you're trying to intimidate me into confessing something," she began, her voice shaky, "you may think again."

"I'm not trying to intimidate you," he murmured, his lips so close to her ear that she could feel the warmth of his breath. "I'm trying to kiss you."

And then, without giving her a chance to respond, he bent his head and claimed her lips.

The first touch of his mouth against hers was soft, tentative, but it sent a rush of heat through her body that left her trembling. It was everything she had imagined it would be—sweet, unbearably sweet—and yet so much more. His hands tightened around her waist, pulling her closer, and for a moment, the world fell away, leaving only the heat of his body, the press of his lips, and the dizzying need building between them.

For Henry, the kiss was everything he had been longing for. He had wanted her since the moment she had burst into his life, standing over him with that ridiculous bed warmer in hand. She had been a temptation from the very start, and now, with her soft body pressed against his and her lips yielding to his, he knew he could never let her go. The taste of her was intoxicating, a promise of pleasures yet to come, and he groaned inwardly as desire surged through him. He wanted to deepen the kiss, to claim her fully, but his honor held him back. She deserved better than to be ravished in a drawing room.

With an effort, he forced himself to pull back, though it nearly killed him to do so.

"I've been wanting to do that ever since I first laid eyes on you," he whispered, brushing a stray curl from her forehead. "You are... an impossible temptation, my sweet."

Rose's cheeks flushed with warmth at his words, and she found herself unable to look him in the eye. She ought to slap him, she knew. A proper lady would. But her heart was still racing, her head spinning from the intensity of his kiss, and she was too disoriented to even think of moving away. Worse still, she realized, was that she didn't want to move away.

"I—"

"No." His voice was gentle but firm as he rested his thumb against her jaw, tilting her face back up to meet his gaze. "I know this shouldn't have happened," he admitted, his thumb tracing slow circles over her heated skin. "But I won't pretend to regret it. And I hope you don't regret it either. Do you?"

Touched by the vulnerability in his words, Rose placed her hand over his, pressing it to her cheek. "I regret nothing," she whispered, her voice soft but sure.

"Good." He exhaled, his eyes darkening once more as his thumb moved over her lips. "I couldn't bear it if you did."

Before she could respond, he dipped his head again, stealing another quick, heated kiss that left her breathless. Then, with what seemed like Herculean effort, he stepped back, his hands clenching at his sides as if to prevent himself from reaching for her again.

"Perhaps," he said hoarsely, "it would be best if we said goodnight." His eyes lingered on her, burning with unspoken desire, before he finally forced himself to look away. "So... will you accompany us to Derby tomorrow?"

It took Rose a moment to process his words, her mind still fogged by the heat of their kiss. "I... I was planning to, yes," she stammered, praying he wouldn't ask her to stay behind. She had to see him again, even if it meant being surrounded by a dozen other people.

He gave a curt nod, his voice still rough with barely restrained passion. "Then I shall see you tomorrow."

"Goodnight, Henry," she whispered, her heart still racing as he turned and walked away, leaving her standing in the middle of the room, feeling as though the ground had shifted beneath her feet.

Rose spent a restless night reliving the kiss, her thoughts spiraling endlessly between the memory of Henry's lips on hers and the way his strong, muscular body had pressed so intimately against her. She shivered as she recalled the heady mix of desire and fear that had nearly overwhelmed her. Thank heavens he'd been noble enough to end the embrace when he had, she mused, turning onto her back with a heavy sigh. The mere thought of what might have happened had he not shown such restraint sent a shudder through her.

It wasn't as if she had never been kissed before, she reassured herself, frowning at the ceiling. She was no wanton, but neither was she completely innocent. There had been a few stolen kisses throughout her girlhood, but none of them had made her forget herself so completely. Henry had stirred something within her that frightened her as much as it excited her—an unrelenting passion she had never known. She feared that she had been on the verge of offering him not just her body, but her heart as well.

When she finally awoke the next morning, Rose was bleary-eyed and tense, her sleep having been too sparse and too filled with the vivid memory of his kiss. She stayed hidden in her study for most of the morning, pretending to work on the final arrangements for the costume ball. Maggie informed her that Henry had gone about his usual morning duties and expected to return by noon. The news allowed her to breathe a small sigh of relief. Perhaps by then, she could school her emotions and face him with some semblance of calm.

They set out for Derby after luncheon, traveling in three separate coaches. In honor of the occasion, Rose wore one of her new gowns—a fetching cherry-red muslin, with a chip straw bonnet adorned with a matching ribbon perched neatly on her curls. A striped parasol and a pair of crocheted mitts completed the ensemble. She felt confident enough to hold her own among the well-dressed beauties. That she cared so much about her appearance left her feeling faintly ashamed, but at least she was finally behaving like a lady. Her father, she thought with a grim smile, would doubtlessly be gratified.

In Derby, they met Miss Felton and Mr. Langford at the cathedral, where they admired the soaring stained-glass windows. But Rose, ever observant, noted that Miss Felton seemed somewhat unsettled. Taking the opportunity for a private word, she gently pulled her aside.

"Is everything all right, Miss Felton?" Rose asked, her voice soft with concern as she studied the other woman's flushed cheeks.

Miss Felton hesitated, her gaze flicking nervously toward Mr. Langford. "I am sorry to be such poor company," she confessed, the color in her cheeks deepening. "But that wretched man has been plaguing me all morning, and I vow, I have reached the end of my patience!"

Rose blinked, startled by the vehemence in her voice. "Indeed?" She glanced sharply at Mr. Langford, narrowing her eyes. "Has he been making untoward advances? If so, I'm certain Lord Ashbourne would have no qualms about speaking to him.

Miss Felton's eyes widened in alarm, her hand flying to her mouth. "Oh, no! It's not that at all!" Her flush darkened as she glanced back at Mr. Langford. "It's simply that he insists on believing I find his attentions flattering when, in truth, he is insufferable! He follows me around like a dog, and I can't shake him!"

Rose raised an eyebrow, suppressing a smile. There was something in Miss Felton's tone—something just beneath the surface—that didn't quite match the indignation in her words. "Are you sure it's only his persistence that troubles you?" she asked, her voice gently teasing. "It seems to me there might be more to it than that."

Miss Felton bit her lip, looking flustered. "I—he's... I suppose he can be charming when he chooses to be," she admitted reluctantly, her chin lifting in defiance of her own feelings. "But it's vexing! He seems to take pleasure in provoking me."

Rose's smile deepened. "Perhaps that is his way of showing affection," she suggested. "Men often do the strangest things when they are interested."

Miss Felton's blush returned in full force, and she looked away, clearly unsettled. "If that is the case, then I wish he would show his interest in some less aggravating manner."

"If he gives you further trouble," Rose said, unable to resist her amusement, "do not hesitate to tell his lordship. He will soon set Mr. Langford straight. Though," she added with a chuckle, "I suspect you might not truly want him to."

Miss Felton's eyes widened again, but this time there was a flicker of something other than irritation—something that made Rose believe the handsome rascal might have a better chance with her than he realized.

"If he continues to vex me," Miss Felton muttered with feeling, "I shall push him off the cathedral tower myself."

Meanwhile, Henry stood nearby, half-listening to Lady Langwick extol the cathedral's stained-glass windows. His gaze, however, remained fixed on Rose. She was standing beneath the stone arches, the colorful light from the windows casting a radiant glow on her pale skin. The sight took his breath away. He had always thought her beautiful, but today... today, she was more than that. She was utterly captivating.

As if sensing his gaze, she glanced up suddenly, their eyes meeting across the room. In that brief moment, the world around them faded, leaving only the two of them. His heart thundered in his chest, and he couldn't tear his eyes away from her. All he could think about was the kiss they had shared the night before.

The taste of her lips lingered on his tongue, sweet and intoxicating. He had spent the entire night haunted by it, replaying it in his mind with increasing frustration. Even as he'd gone about his morning duties, the memory had clung to him, making his breeches uncomfortably tight as his desire for her simmered beneath the surface. Ending the kiss had been one of the hardest things he had ever done, and he'd had to call upon every shred of his self-control to pull back before he lost himself entirely.

He clenched his jaw, his body tense with the effort of restraint. If he had kissed her any longer, he wasn't sure he would have been able to stop. But he had—because he was a gentleman. And though he regretted nothing about that kiss, he knew he had to be careful. The next time, he wasn't sure he could be so noble.

As Rose dropped her gaze and turned away, her cheeks pink, Henry felt a powerful surge of emotion—a mix of longing and frustration that made him want to cross the room and take her in his arms again. But before he could act on the impulse, another group of visitors entered the cloister, their voices cutting through the spell.

"My heavens, Lord Ashbourne! Is that you?" A woman's voice cut through his thoughts, sharp as a blade.

Henry's blood ran cold. That voice. His muscles tensed as a deep, familiar bitterness surged through him. Slowly, he turned to face the speaker, dread pooling in his chest.

Standing before him was a striking woman, her indigo eyes gleaming with playful mischief and the same bright, mocking smile he remembered all too well.

Carla.

His heart hammered in his chest as the memories came flooding back—the humiliation, the laughter, the cruel nickname she had flung at him in front of everyone at Almack's. "The Ox from Oxford." The shame had seared him, and that moment had shaped so much of the man he had become.

"Do you recognize me?" Carla asked, her voice as light and confident as ever. "It's Carla! What are you doing here?"

Chapter Eighteen

Henry's jaw clenched as emotions surged through him—a bitter mix of anger and an old, raw vulnerability he'd long despised. Carla Witherspoon—no, Lady Dumfries—had once been the object of his affection. She'd captivated him as a youth, until she publicly humiliated him and shattered his illusions of love, honor, and society.

At first, he couldn't believe it was truly her standing before him. For years, he'd imagined how he would react if their paths crossed again. He'd pictured himself composed, clever, indifferent. But now, confronted by her in the flesh, all he could do was stare. The icy numbness that had settled over him threatened to betray his calm demeanor, and aware that he had become the object of the everyone's attention, Henry forced himself to recover.

"Good afternoon, Lady Dumfries," he said, managing a polite bow despite the tension in his voice. "I hadn't heard you were in the area. I trust you are well?"

Her eyes, once as blue as the sapphires he had foolishly compared them to in his youth, sparked with amusement. "Oh, Henry," she cooed, her lips curling into a playful smile, "I hardly know how to answer that. I am quite well, but I fear my poor husband is not. He passed away more than a year ago."

Henry felt the heat of embarrassment rise to his cheeks, taking him back to the awkwardness of his youth. "I see," he murmured, his cravat suddenly feeling like a noose around his neck. "My condolences, my lady."

"You are too kind," she replied with a lazy wave of her fan, her voice dripping with false modesty. "But it has been some time, and I have come to terms with being alone. And what of you, Henry? What brings you to Derby, and in such lively company? I had heard you had become something of a recluse, rarely seen outside your estate."

Rose, who had been watching this exchange with increasing discomfort, took the opportunity to step forward, her tone crisp. "His lordship has been kind enough to show us around the town," she said, her voice cutting through the air like a blade.

Carla's gaze flicked to Rose, and her eyes narrowed ever so slightly. "Is he indeed?" she purred, the sound more serpent than woman. "How fortunate for you, Miss...?"

"Miss Sheffield," Rose supplied, meeting the marchioness's gaze with cool composure.

"Ah," Carla said softly, her smile sharpening. "In that case, perhaps you wouldn't mind if my friends and I joined your party? The day has been frightfully dull."

The three dandies trailing behind Carla exchanged uneasy glances, and the ladies with them shifted uncomfortably. The marchioness had clearly made herself unwelcome, but there was no graceful way to refuse her without causing a scene. Before Rose could think of a proper reply, Carla wound her arm through Henry's, claiming him with the casual arrogance of a woman who had never been denied.

"Forward creature," Rose heard Lady Langwick mutter to one of the other mothers. "It would seem the rumors are true after all. Quite bold, isn't she?"

"One hates to speak ill of the dead," Mrs. Darlington murmured primly, though her satisfaction was barely concealed. "But I've heard her late husband not only tolerated her antics but encouraged them. My husband says the marquis even indulged her indiscretions, and..." she lowered her voice, "there were... others."

Rose bit back a groan of frustration. Normally, she had no taste for gossip, but something about Lady Dumfries made her want to learn every last scandalous detail. Perhaps it was the way she flitted between men, flirting openly with both Mr. Langford and Henry, clinging to the latter with possessive arrogance. The sight made Rose's hands clench around her parasol. How she longed to box the woman's ears or, at the very least, knock that smug smile off her face.

While Rose fumed, Henry was lost in his own troubled thoughts. The shock of seeing Carla again was beginning to wear off, and as it did, his emotions shifted. Where once he might have been consumed by anger or even longing, now he felt only a dull indifference—and perhaps a faint sense of relief. Time and distance had shown him the truth of Carla's nature. She was beautiful, yes, but cold and calculating. Thank God she had rejected him all those years ago. He shuddered to think what life might have been like as her husband.

"You're rather quiet, my lord," Carla's voice slithered into his thoughts, her hand tightening on his arm. "What are you thinking?"

Henry glanced down at her, his eyes cool. For a brief moment, he considered answering her honestly, telling her exactly what he thought of her now. But years of hard-won self-control held him in check.

"I was thinking, my lady, that I ought to visit Derby more often," he said smoothly, his gaze sliding away from hers. "This is my first time visiting the cathedral since my father's death."

Carla's lips pursed in mild disappointment. "I hear there is to be an assembly tomorrow night," she ventured, her voice taking on a bored tone. "Country entertainments can be so dreadfully dull, but if you are attending, perhaps I shall come along as well." She shot him a languid look, her lashes sweeping low. "I'm sure we could find ways to keep each other entertained."

Henry remembered the days when a single glance from those sapphire eyes would have undone him. Now, he felt nothing. Well, almost nothing. It amused him to see how desperate she was to regain his favor—a far cry from the haughty girl who had spurned him so cruelly.

"As host, I fear I shall be occupied with my guests," he replied lightly. "But I'm sure I can make time for an old friend."

Carla's smile faltered for a split second before she recovered, her laugh bright and artificial. "I would much rather you refer to me as a *dear* friend," she corrected, batting her lashes. "After all, 'old friend' sounds so dreadfully antiquated, don't you agree?"

Henry's smile sharpened. "As if anyone could ever mistake you for anything less than a fresh-faced debutante," he retorted, surprised at how easily the words came. It was Rose's influence, he realized. Her wit had sharpened his own, and for the first time, he felt as though he had truly stepped out of the shadow of his youthful insecurities.

Without realizing it, Rose had taught him to lower the walls he had built around his heart, and rather than feeling exposed or vulnerable, he felt free. The realization filled him with a sudden desire to return to Thornfield—to be near her again. But first, he needed to extricate himself from Carla's clutches.

He was searching for an excuse when one of Carla's dandies, Sir Charles Chesterfield, stepped forward, reminding her stiffly that they were expected elsewhere for tea. The glance Carla shot him was withering, but when she turned back to Henry, her smile was all sweetness.

"Duty calls," she said, extending her hand to him. "I shall look forward to seeing you tomorrow evening."

Henry's eyes gleamed with cool amusement as he bent over her hand. "As shall I, Lady Dumfries," he murmured smoothly. "As shall I."

They returned to Thornfield Hall in far lower spirits than when they'd set out, and Rose wasn't the least bit surprised when half the guests claimed sudden headaches and retreated to their rooms. Heaven knew she was tempted to feign a similar malady, but as Lady Dumfries had so glibly reminded her, duty called. Rose paused just long enough to wash her face and hands before hurrying down to the parlor, where Lady Beatrice sat, impatience etched into her features.

"Well?" the countess demanded the moment Rose entered. "Did Henry single out any lady for his attentions?

"You might say that," Rose replied, sinking wearily into a chair across from her. "He showed a marked preference for one lady in particular. I saw him kiss her hand at least twice."

"Twice?" Lady Beatrice's eyes gleamed. "Was it that charming Miss Felton? Didn't I say they would suit each other perfectly?"

"So you did." Rose sighed. "But no, Miss Felton was not the object of his lordship's favor."

The countess's brow furrowed. "He wasn't making up to one of those Darlington girls, was he?" she asked, scowling. "They're sweet enough, but far too young. I would not have it said that Henry plucked his bride straight from the nursery."

An ironic smile tugged at Rose's lips. "Indeed not," she assured her, her voice quiet but steady. "The lady in question is rather closer to his own age."

"Really?" Lady Beatrice's eyes narrowed, perplexed. "I don't recall anyone of suitable years, unless..." She trailed off, her eyes flashing with sudden horror. "Surely he wasn't dangling after one of the mamas?"

Rose almost laughed at the thought of Henry chasing Lady Langwick about the cloisters, but her amusement was fleeting. "No, my lady," she said softly.

"Then blast it all, who was it?" Lady Beatrice snapped, her patience unraveling.

"Lady Carla Dumfries."

The color drained from Lady Beatrice's face, her hands flying to her throat. "What?" she gasped, staring at Rose as if she'd uttered the most unspeakable of obscenities. "No, it cannot be. If you're playing me false, Rose, I vow I'll be quite cross with you."

Rose let out a heavy sigh. "I'm not jesting, my lady. I wish I were." She proceeded to recount every painful detail of the encounter, her voice dull with fatigue.

When she finished, Lady Beatrice sat motionless, her face a mask of horror. "And you say my son *encouraged* this... this hussy?" Her voice trembled with fury. "I refuse to believe it! He cannot be so lacking in pride."

"I told you we should have warned him of the marchioness's presence," Rose murmured unhappily. "If he'd known she was near, he might have been able to steel himself. But as it was, she simply appeared before him, and—"

Lady Beatrice bristled at the faint accusation, her eyes flashing. "I fail to see how it would have made a difference," she said stiffly. "If he is as besotted with the woman as you say, it would hardly have mattered."

"I didn't say he was besotted," Rose countered, her voice catching as a sharp, unexpected pain gripped her chest. Only last night, Henry had kissed her with such fervor, had held her as if she were the only woman in the world. And now... he seemed to have forgotten her very existence. Oh, he had been polite enough on the ride back from Derby, but his mood had been brooding and distracted. It didn't take much imagination to guess who had occupied his thoughts. The knowledge made her throat tighten with unshed tears.

"...you're going through," the countess concluded with a weary sigh, her voice pulling Rose from her thoughts.

"I beg your pardon, my lady?" Rose asked, blinking away the sting in her eyes.

"I said," Lady Beatrice repeated patiently, "that for all his faults, my son is no fool. He may think he's in love with her as he was in his youth, but once he sees Lady Dumfries for what she is—a scheming, heartless little jade—he will realize it's nothing more than the last embers of a long-dead flame."

Rose wished she could believe that. But she knew Henry too well. He wasn't a callow boy anymore, easily swayed by fleeting passions. He was a man of conviction, and when he gave his heart, it was a deliberate, irrevocable act. The thought made her hands tremble, and the delicate china cup rattled on its saucer.

"My word, Rose, are you unwell?" Lady Beatrice asked, her sharp eyes narrowing in concern. "You've gone pale."

"It's nothing, my lady," Rose replied, forcing a smile as she carefully set the cup aside. "Just a slight headache."

"Then you must go to your room at once," Lady Beatrice declared with authority. "You should never have come down in the first place."

"But the guests—"

"Oh, nonsense!" the countess interrupted with a dismissive wave. "I've been managing guests since before you were in leading strings. Besides," she added with a wry smile, "your headache seems to be contagious. Half the house has retired early."

Rose didn't bother responding to the jibe. "If you're certain it won't be an inconvenience," she said, rising from her chair, "I'd be grateful for the rest."

"Go on, child," Lady Beatrice said, patting her hand kindly. "If anything goes awry, I'll send for Henry. It's about time he started doing his duty by his guests."

Rose blinked back the tears that threatened to spill at the countess's unexpected kindness. "You're too good to me, my lady," she murmured, bending to press a light kiss to the older woman's cheek. "Good afternoon."

Lady Beatrice watched her go, her own eyes misting. As soon as she was alone, she pulled out the small portrait of her late husband, which hung from a chain around her neck. "Blast it, Ashbourne," she muttered, frowning at the miniature of his painted face. "What are we going to do now?"

Chapter Nineteen

"So this is where you've been hiding yourself," Henry teased, his voice light but laced with an undercurrent of something deeper as he came upon Rose picking flowers the following afternoon. He hadn't realized just how much he'd been searching for her until now, his heart unexpectedly lifting at the sight of her. She wore a simple gown of lavender and cream silk, the soft hues complementing the basket of blooms she carried, and he found himself thinking she looked as lovely as the roses in her grasp.

"Good afternoon, my lord," she replied, her tone as cool and contrasting as her warm eyes that peeked up at him from beneath the wide brim of her straw bonnet. "Was there something you wanted?"

The formal address, as well as the chill in her voice, made his brow lift in surprise. "For starters, you might call me Henry," he said, reminding her gently of the promise she'd made not so long ago. Without waiting for permission, he reached out, plucking the rose she had just cut from her fingers. Holding her gaze, he brought the bloom to his nose, inhaling its sweet fragrance before kissing its soft petals, then handing it back to her in silence.

To his delight, the gesture did not go unnoticed. Her cheeks flushed the softest shade of pink. "As you wish... Henry," she murmured, quickly turning her attention back to the flowers, her hands suddenly busy. "Is there anything else you needed? Lady Langwick is quite anxious that I finish cutting these flowers by mid-afternoon. We've bouquets to make for all the ladies, you see."

Henry felt a flicker of frustration. Only two nights ago, they had been in each other's arms, locked in a passionate embrace. Now, she was treating him as though he were no more than a casual acquaintance. The sudden distance between them made him want to pull her back into his arms, to remind her that he was far more than that, but reason told him this was neither the time nor the place. Not that he intended to let the matter rest unchallenged. Quietly, he removed the clippers from her fingers and snipped a single white rose.

"Will you be attending the assembly with us?" he asked, twirling the flower between his thumb and forefinger.

Her brow furrowed in confusion. "Of course," she replied, her tone clipped. "You made me promise to waltz with you, remember?"

"I do," he answered, his voice low, almost husky. "But I thought perhaps you might have forgotten... along with a few other things."

Her eyes narrowed at the veiled remark. "What other things?"

He only smiled at her soft, indignant demand. "I'll tell you later," he promised, cutting her off before she could press further. "What color is your ball gown?"

"My gown?" She blinked, momentarily thrown by the change in topic. "It's ruby. Why?"

"Then wear this," he said, handing her the dew-dappled blossom.

Rose accepted the rose with a skeptical frown. "And why should I?"

"For effect, for one thing," he replied, the corner of his mouth curving upward in amusement at her obvious suspicion. "The contrast will be stunning."

"And the other reason?" she asked, her voice sharper now, pressing him when he did not elaborate.

"It will tell me that you're thinking about me," he said softly, his tone suddenly serious, "as I will be thinking about you."

Without warning, he caught her hand in his and brought it to his lips for a kiss, lingering just long enough for the gesture to make her breath hitch.

Their eyes met, and in the golden depths of hers, he saw the same turmoil and unspoken desire that had been tormenting him for days. His fingers tightened around hers, and for one reckless moment, he was tempted to cast aside his restraint, to pull her into his arms and kiss her senseless, consequences be damned. But something—honor, or perhaps self-preservation—held him back, and with a quiet sigh, he released her hand, already feeling the weight of regret settle over him.

He stepped back, leaving her standing among the flowers, a faint blush still coloring her cheeks. He had no idea where they stood, only that he felt more alone and conflicted than ever before.

After retreating from the gardens, Rose retired to her room, her mind swirling with thoughts of Henry's behavior. She was furious—furious with him for his shameless flirting, but even more furious with herself for being so easily captivated by his polished charm. Until yesterday, he had been the last man she would have labeled a rake, but now? Now, she wasn't so certain. Surely only a man of low principles would kiss one woman in the moonlight and then court the attentions of his lost love the very next day. The thought brought a shimmer of tears to her eyes as she gazed out of the window.

Lost love. The term made her wince. When Henry had kissed her, had he been thinking of Lady Dumfries? Perhaps if he'd known she was in the area, newly widowed and free from her former marriage, he would never have touched her—never have kissed *her*, Rose. But even her logical mind couldn't make sense of his actions this afternoon. He had known about Lady Dumfries, yet he had still kissed her hand, his eyes betraying a desire she could scarcely comprehend.

Did he truly care for her? Or was he merely toying with her, as men of his rank so often did with women beneath their station? The question gnawed at her, twisting painfully in her heart. She wished she knew the answer, and she wished, even more fervently, that she knew what on earth she was going to do about it.

She was still no closer to solving this puzzle when Maggie entered, bustling in to help her dress for dinner.

"Becoming a regular lady of society, aren't you?" Maggie scolded good-naturedly as she set to work arranging Rose's dark hair into a neat coil at the back of her head. "Taking to your room with a headache every afternoon, and then drifting about pale and delicate like one of them ladies who always has a bottle of smelling salts on hand. You'll be swooning next, mark my words."

"Don't lecture, Maggie," Rose murmured, barely glancing at her reflection. She had been eagerly anticipating the assembly ever since it had been mentioned, but now? Now she wondered if she could beg off. She wasn't sure she could endure watching Henry waltzing with the marchioness, all smiles and whispered confidences.

"If I didn't lecture you, you'd be worse off for it," Maggie sniffed, picking up a necklace of delicate gold filigree, set with rubies, and fastening it around Rose's neck. "A young woman needs a bit of prompting now and then, and it's my duty to see you get it."

"A duty you seem to relish," Rose muttered, though there was no real venom in her voice.

"Don't be saucy. You know well enough I only have your best interests at heart," Maggie replied, deftly fixing matching ruby earrings in place. Stepping back, she surveyed her handiwork with a critical eye. "There now, you look a fine sight if I do say so myself. I heard Lady Langwick suggested you wear one of them dreadful turban things, but I'm glad to see you paid her no mind. You've lovely hair, and it'd be a shame to hide it."

The mention of Lady Langwick made Rose's lips curve in a small, wry smile, remembering their conversation that afternoon.

"Of course, there is nothing so sad as a lady who refuses to accept the inevitability of her years," Lady Langwick had declared, fixing Rose with a pointed look. "Unmarried ladies of a certain age should accept their fate and wear the caps and turbans that society deems proper for a spinster. It is far more dignified than clinging to girlish curls, don't you agree, Miss Sheffield?"

Rose had been feeling rather low at the time, nursing her own sorrows, but Lady Langwick's pompous remark had been exactly what she needed to snap her out of it. There was nothing Rose enjoyed more than deflating such pretentious airs. She had taken a delicate sip of tea, smiling sweetly as she replied, "Indeed I do, my lady. And I'm glad to see your daughter follows your excellent advice. That's a lovely cap you're wearing, Lady Margaret," she'd added with the faintest hint of malice.

"This is not a cap," Lady Margaret had huffed, her face reddening. "It's a French chapeau, and it's all the rage in London!"

"My mistake then," Rose had replied with feigned sweetness, feeling a delicious satisfaction until she'd caught sight of Henry across the room.

His expression had been carefully neutral, but his eyes had danced with silent laughter. He'd raised his teacup in a mock salute, and for a brief, perfect moment, Rose had felt a closeness to him stronger than anything they'd shared before.

The memory of that shared moment now made her breath catch. She stared into the mirror, her pulse quickening, as the truth finally dawned on her. She loved Henry.

"Good evening, Miss Sheffield. That is a beautiful gown you are wearing."

The gentle voice pierced through Rose's reverie. She glanced up from the bench where she had sought refuge and found Miss Felton standing before her. For a fleeting moment, she was tempted to ask the young lady—whom she had come to regard as a friend—to leave her in peace. But good manners prevailed over her desire for solitude, and she managed a weak smile.

"Thank you, Miss Felton," she said quietly, sliding over on the bench to make room. "Might I say you look lovely yourself?"

"If you like," Lydia replied with a rustle of powder-blue silk as she arranged herself next to Rose. When she was satisfied with the drape of her skirts, she turned to Rose with a warm smile. "Now that we've dispensed with pleasantries, I wish you would call me Lydia. And your name is Rose, is it not?"

Rose nodded, touched by the offer of friendship. "Father named me for Shakespeare's Rosalind," she explained, her lips curving slightly at the memory. "He was a literature lecturer at Cambridge and was teaching As You Like It when my mother gave birth to me. I've often been grateful that he wasn't lecturing on Titus Andronicus at the time."

Lydia chuckled. "A fortunate turn of fate, indeed. Although…" Her gaze flitted toward Lady Dumfries. "What do you suppose Shakespeare would have made of our merry widow?"

Rose reluctantly followed Lydia's gaze. "Something scathing, no doubt," she said, glancing away quickly. "He had an eye for characters like her."

"And a pen to match," Lydia added, unfurling her fan and waving it delicately. "Mr. Langford told me she was the Duke of Edinburgh's mistress until he tossed her aside when she pressed him for marriage."

Rose was unsurprised by the news, having already taken the widow's measure with a single glance. What did surprise her, however, was that Mr. Langford had shared such a scandalous detail with Lydia. She toyed with her own fan before replying.

"That sounds like something no gentleman should share with a lady," she remarked, her gaze fixed on Lydia with gentle reproach.

To her astonishment, Lydia blushed. "It was my fault, really," she confessed, her eyes dropping to her hands. "I scolded him for allowing such an obvious flirt to wrap him around her finger. He assured me I had nothing to fear—he had no intention of offering for… well… 'shopworn goods,' as he put it."

Rose blinked at the cruel phrase, but before she could press Lydia further, a shadow fell over them. She glanced up, and her heart stopped when she saw Henry standing before her.

"I've come to claim my waltz," he said in that deep, familiar voice. "You did promise it to me, after all."

As if she could ever forget. Rose's thoughts churned as she gazed up at him, committing every detail of his face to memory. Had she loved him even then, when he first took her into his arms? The question filled her mind with painful confusion.

"Rose?" His brows furrowed in puzzlement. "Do you no longer wish to waltz?"

His question startled her out of her thoughts, and she rose quickly to her feet. After murmuring a polite apology to Lydia, she allowed Henry to lead her onto the dance floor, where couples were already gathering in anticipation.

He slid a firm arm around her waist, his hand enveloping hers as they waited for the music to begin. "I see you're wearing my rose," he murmured, his voice low as he drew her closer. "I'm glad."

Rose was determined not to be charmed by his words. "As you said, it complements my gown," she replied stiffly, making an attempt to pull away.

He didn't allow her to, holding her even closer. "I meant to tell you," he whispered as they began to glide across the room in time with the lilting music, "that you look incredibly beautiful tonight. I half expected I would have to battle through a legion of suitors to claim my waltz."

Rose, who had spent more time on her bench than on the dance floor, saw through the flattery immediately. She lifted her face to his, ready to scold him for uttering such nonsense. But when their eyes met, she faltered. There was something in his gaze that confused her, something almost... sincere. If she hadn't seen him earlier, dancing with Lady Dumfries, she might have believed that he was captivated by her. She quickly dismissed the notion as foolish.

She had to remind herself that Henry Ashbourne was a rake—a man not to be trusted. If she had known that taming him would lead to this, she never would have tried.

While Rose inwardly berated herself for her foolishness, Henry's thoughts were equally tangled. He had spent the better part of the evening in Lady Dumfries' company, and with each passing moment, he had questioned how he had ever believed himself in love with her. She was as spiteful as he remembered, her conversation shallow and self-absorbed. She clung to him, brazen and suggestive, as though she expected him to fall back into her arms without hesitation.

But through it all, his thoughts had remained on Rose. As beautiful as Lady Dumfries appeared in her daring gold-shot silk gown, it was Rose, in her simple, modest dress, who had truly captured his attention. And where Carla's conversation had bored him to the point of stifling yawns, Rose's quick wit and intelligence had stirred something far deeper in him.

It was a wonder to him now, that he had ever considered a life with Carla. How could he have been so blind? The entire time he had been with her, his thoughts had been elsewhere—on Rose.

He chuckled softly to himself, the absurdity of the situation washing over him.

Rose frowned at the sound. "Does something amuse you, my lord?" she asked coolly, her voice edged with frost.

Henry's smile widened, thoroughly enjoying the fire in her eyes. "A great many things," he replied, leaning in slightly, his gaze intent. He was on the verge of suggesting a stroll on the balcony when the master of ceremonies rushed up to them, his face pale with worry.

"Lord Ashbourne! Lord Ashbourne!" the man exclaimed, his voice breathless. "You must come at once—your mother has collapsed!"

Chapter Twenty

"I wish everyone would stop fussing and leave me be!" Lady Beatrice's voice echoed through the ballroom as Rose and Henry hurried toward the small crowd gathered around her. Henry roughly pushed one man aside, his face pale with concern as he knelt beside his mother.

"Are you all right?" he asked, his voice gentle despite the tightness in his chest as he took her hand. "What happened?"

"It was the silliest thing, really," Lady Beatrice muttered, looking more embarrassed than injured. "I dropped my reticule, and when I leaned over to pick it up, I tumbled out of my chair. Now help me up, for heaven's sake. This blasted floor is like ice."

The impatient demand eased Henry's initial fear, and he bent to help her to her feet. He was halfway through lifting her when she gave a sharp cry.

"My leg!"

He set her down carefully, stepping back in alarm. "What is it?" he asked, his eyes full of concern as he knelt beside her once more.

"It's tingling, like it's on fire," she grumbled, her lips twisting into a grimace as she rubbed the affected limb. "I've had the odd twinge before, but nothing like this. I must've jolted it when I fell."

Rose, standing close by, had been ready to assist but took a step back at the countess's words. So *this* was the miraculous recovery she'd hinted at. Admiration for the older woman's craftiness dispelled Rose's lingering concern, though she knew there would be time later to take Lady Beatrice to task for her theatrics. For now, it was best to get her home before she conjured up more mischief.

"Perhaps we should take you back to Thornfield," Rose suggested, placing a steadying hand on Henry's arm. "We can have the doctor meet us there."

Henry, who hadn't considered calling a doctor until Rose mentioned it, nodded sharply. He ordered a footman to fetch the physician, then turned back to his mother. After a brief discussion, it was agreed that those guests who wished to stay at the assembly would remain, while the rest prepared to depart for Thornfield. Less than ten minutes later, they were on their way back to the estate.

Henry sat across from his mother in the carriage, his face tight with worry, unaware that he was crushing Rose's fingers in his grip. The image of Lady Beatrice sprawled on the ballroom floor kept flashing through his mind, a painful reminder of the accident that had first injured her. It was his fault—all of it. The guilt gnawed at him, threatening to overwhelm him.

"Henry?"

Rose's soft voice pierced through his fog of despair, and he glanced down to find her watching him with concern. It was only then that he realized how tightly he was holding her hand. He quickly loosened his grip, his thumb brushing over her knuckles as though trying to soothe the pain.

"Was I hurting you?" His voice was gruff with regret. "I'm sorry—I sometimes forget my own strength."

"You weren't hurting me," Rose lied, though her fingers throbbed in protest. "I was just going to say that you needn't look so grim. Everything will be all right."

When she smiled at him like that, Henry found it impossible not to believe her. "I know," he said softly, lifting her hand to his lips and pressing a tender kiss to her knuckles. Their eyes met, and in that moment, he felt a rush of gratitude and something more—something deeper—that made him wish they were anywhere but in this crowded carriage.

Whatever he might have said next was cut short by Lady Beatrice's sudden, imperious voice from across the seat.

"What are you two whispering about over there?" she demanded, her tone sharp. "There's no need to be so secretive—I'm not on my deathbed, you know!"

Henry and Rose exchanged amused glances. "We know you're not, Mother," Henry replied with a chuckle. "We just didn't want to disturb you with idle conversation."

"Conversation, is it?" Lady Beatrice sniffed in disbelief. "Is that what they call it these days?"

In less than half an hour, they arrived back at Thornfield. Henry carried his mother upstairs, depositing her in her room before leaving her to Rose and the ever-efficient Mabel. Once Lady Beatrice had been undressed and made as comfortable as possible, the doctor arrived to examine her. Henry, much as he hated being gently ushered from the room, accepted it with resignation and retreated downstairs to wait.

In the drawing room, he paced restlessly, his mind racing. He was considering ringing for brandy when the door opened, and Rose stepped in.

"How is she?" he asked urgently, crossing the room in three quick strides to grab her hand. "Is she all right? It's not her heart, is it?"

"No, nothing like that," Rose assured him, though inside she was seething at Lady Beatrice for putting such fear in his eyes. She had already taken the countess to task in private for her theatrical display, but now she regretted not being sterner. Whatever Lady Beatrice's motives, she had no right to put her son through such unnecessary torment.

"Thank God," Henry breathed, closing his eyes in relief. He'd sensed that his mother was keeping something from him, and the fear of her being more ill than she let on had gnawed at him for days. When he opened his eyes again, his gaze softened as it rested on Rose.

"What did the doctor say?" he asked, leading her over to one of the settees and sitting beside her, still holding her hand as though it were a lifeline.

"He's still examining her, but he doesn't seem overly concerned," Rose replied, her guilt weighing heavier than ever. She loved Henry, and being forced to deceive him was tearing her apart. But she'd given her word, and no matter how distasteful she found the duplicity, she felt bound by it. "In fact," she added, "he seemed... encouraged."

"Encouraged?" Henry frowned. "That's an odd choice of word."

Rose shifted uncomfortably under his gaze, wishing he wasn't sitting so close. "He... he believes the tingling in her legs may be a sign that feeling is returning to them," she said at last, grateful that in this, at least, she could speak the truth.

"Do you mean she could walk again?" Henry asked, his voice incredulous.

The happiness in his tone only deepened Rose's misery. "The doctor didn't say that outright," she replied, her voice quiet. "But it seems a logical conclusion."

"That's wonderful!" Henry exclaimed, pulling her into an exuberant hug. When she didn't respond, he drew back, confusion clouding his expression. "You don't seem very happy about it," he noted, his eyes narrowing in suspicion.

Rose flinched at his perception. "Of course, I'm happy," she said, forcing a weak smile as she averted her eyes. "I suppose the news hasn't quite sunk in yet. I've been so worried for so long..." Her laugh sounded hollow, even to her own ears.

Henry gave her a sharp look, about to press further, when the doctor entered the room, saving her from further scrutiny. Henry immediately rose to his feet, still gripping Rose's hand.

"How is my mother?" he asked, bracing himself for the answer.

"Better than I've seen her in years, my lord!" the elderly physician replied, his lined face lighting up with a broad smile. "All feeling has returned to her ladyship's legs, and with time, I believe she may walk again. A miracle, that's what it is—a true miracle!"

The news of Lady Ashbourne's miraculous recovery spread through the neighborhood faster than a summer storm, and soon Thornfield Hall was overrun with visitors, each more determined than the last to catch a glimpse of the revived invalid. No sooner had one group of curious well-wishers been ushered out the door than another swept in, full of eager questions and exclamations of divine intervention. By mid-afternoon of the second day, Rose's patience had frayed to its very last thread. After finally managing to chase off a particularly persistent group of church ladies from Derbyshire, who had insisted on praying over Lady Beatrice as if she were on her deathbed, Rose collapsed onto the nearest settee with a groan.

"Well, I hope you're satisfied," she muttered, casting a half-hearted glare at the countess, who was reclining with an air of serene contentment. "You'd think this place was Westminster Abbey, the way people have been filing through. A pity we didn't think to charge admission. We'd be quite wealthy by now."

"Don't be vulgar, my dear," Lady Beatrice replied, fanning herself with her usual calm grace. "I've lived in Derbyshire for decades—it's only natural my neighbors would be concerned about my health." She paused, a speculative gleam in her eye. "Although... how much do you think we could charge?"

Rose groaned, cursing herself for having planted the idea in the countess's head. "Never mind that," she muttered. "I still can't believe you pulled something so melodramatic. What on earth were you thinking? We agreed you would recover *naturally*."

Lady Beatrice raised an imperious brow, looking entirely too pleased with herself. "I did recover naturally. What could be more natural than being cured by the grace of God?"

Rose pressed her lips together, trying to stifle the urge to argue. "But—"

"I merely took advantage of my own clumsiness," the countess continued, unperturbed. "You don't honestly think I meant to fall out of that blasted chair, do you?"

Rose blinked, her irritation momentarily giving way to surprise. "You mean to say it was an accident?"

"Of course it was an accident," Lady Beatrice huffed. "I may be many things, but I was raised better than to make a spectacle of myself on purpose."

Rose softened instantly. "I'm sorry. I didn't mean to insult you."

"Well, no harm done," the countess sniffed, though her air of injury lingered for another beat before she dismissed it with a wave of her fan. "In fact, it may have all worked out for the best. At least it managed to divert attention from Henry and *that woman*."

Rose didn't need to ask who *that woman* was. The image of Henry smiling at Lady Dumfries, speaking to her in that soft, teasing way, was still burned in her mind. It took every ounce of effort not to dwell on it now.

"Besides," Lady Beatrice added, her eyes gleaming with renewed vigor, "soon the rest of our guests will arrive, and this whole episode will be nothing more than a passing curiosity. I'll even be able to participate properly—perhaps I'll even dance."

Her tone was cheerful, but Rose couldn't bring herself to share in the countess's optimism. They continued chatting idly for a few more minutes before their solitude was interrupted by the return of Lady Langwick and the rest of the guests, who had been off enjoying an impromptu tour of the countryside. Rose had just started to rise from her seat when she noticed Henry trailing behind them, his dark eyes sweeping the room.

He bent to kiss his mother's cheek, exchanging a few words with her, but then, much to Rose's shock, he turned to her and pressed a kiss to her hand as well.

"Good afternoon, Miss Sheffield," he murmured, his voice warm enough to send a flutter of alarm through her chest. "Hard at work as usual. We must take care that you don't exhaust yourself."

She would not be charmed, Rose told herself firmly. *Not again*. She refused to let herself be swayed by his easy charm, not after what she'd seen with Lady Dumfries. "This, from the man who kept us waiting for dinner while he was off rescuing a sheep from a hedgerow?" she replied archly, slipping her hand free from his grasp.

To her dismay, he let her go with a smile but, instead of moving on, he settled into the chair beside her.

"Oh, but that was last week," Henry said with an easy grin, crossing one booted foot over the other as he leaned back in his chair, his tone teasing. He had spent the entire afternoon waiting to see Rose again, and now that she was here, he couldn't help but take her in.

She was wearing a gown of delicate muslin in a soft, misty rose color that made her skin glow like candlelight. Her hair was arranged in an elegant knot, but he remembered how it had felt between his fingers, the silky strands slipping through his hands. The thought alone stirred a dangerous heat low in his belly, and though he was somewhat embarrassed by his reaction, he couldn't deny the rush of relief it brought him.

The other evening, Carla had pressed herself against him, a deliberate, sensuous provocation meant to incite desire. But he hadn't felt so much as a flicker of interest. The memory had unsettled him, but now, as he watched Rose, he thought he finally understood. His tastes had refined over the years. Thank God for that, he mused, his grin broadening.

Around them, the rest of the company continued their chatter, oblivious to the tension simmering just beneath the surface. Lady Langwick, having evidently given up hope of making a match between Henry and her daughter, had turned her attention to one of the young gentlemen who had been invited to round out the numbers

"The nephew of Lord Mayfield, you know," she confided to Rose in a smug aside. "Rumor has it he'll be named heir, once it's certain his son is dead."

The remark startled Rose enough to make her forget her own swirling emotions. "Once it's *certain* he's dead?" she echoed, frowning. "Surely there wouldn't be any doubt? A man is either dead or he's not. How could there be uncertainty?"

"Because Adrian—his name was Adrian—was reported lost at sea when his ship sank off the Indies," Lady Langwick explained with a patronizing sniff. "Which only proves why an only son should never be allowed to gallivant about the globe. It was the height of selfishness to put his own pleasures above his duty to his family. Don't you agree, my lord?" She turned toward Henry with a smile she no doubt thought was charming.

But Henry's expression darkened, his eyes hardening as he recalled Adrian Comrow. They had been at Oxford together, Adrian two years his junior, but he had admired the young man's fierce intelligence and his resolve to restore his family's fortunes. It had been that very devotion that led to his death, not the foolishness Lady Langwick implied.

"Actually," Henry said, his tone clipped as he fixed the marchioness with an icy stare, "it was his devotion to duty that led to his demise. The Comrows were on the brink of financial ruin before Adrian took to 'gallivanting,' as you call it."

Lady Langwick flushed a deep red, clearly stung by the rebuke, but the arrival of the tea tray mercifully kept the conversation from souring further. The chatter turned to lighter topics, and when the room settled back into its customary hum of conversation, Rose decided it was time to slip away. She couldn't bear another moment in Henry's company, not when his nearness made her heart pound in such a reckless, dangerous way.

She waited until he was engaged in conversation with one of the young men, then quietly rose from her seat and slipped toward the door. But just as she thought she had made her escape, a firm hand closed around her elbow, halting her in her tracks.

"Where are you going?" Henry's voice was soft, but it thrummed with an intensity that sent a shiver down her spine.

She turned to face him, her heart hammering against her ribs as she grasped for an excuse. "I—I need to speak with the housekeeper," she stammered, furious with herself for sounding so flustered. "If Mr.

Granger is truly to be named heir, he should have a proper room. There will be some rearranging to do."

Henry raised an eyebrow, clearly unimpressed by her explanation. "If Granger doesn't care for his quarters, he's welcome to sleep in the stables," he said dismissively. "Besides, I wouldn't be so quick to write off Adrian. If there was any way to survive that shipwreck, he would have found it."

Rose had no response to that, her excuse having already crumbled under his scrutiny. She tried to step back, but his hand remained firmly on her arm, holding her in place. Panic flared in her chest, and she quickly searched for another reason to escape his presence.

"As you say, my lord," she murmured, inclining her head in what she hoped was a polite dismissal. "In that case, I'll need to check on the costumes in the attic. I've arranged for some of our guests to use them."

The use of his title, coupled with her obvious desperation to get away, flicked at Henry's pride like a match to tinder. For a moment, he was sorely tempted to haul her into his arms and kiss her senseless, propriety be damned. But reason prevailed, reminding him that such an impulsive act would ruin her—and his own honor—beyond repair. With an effort, he loosened his grip, releasing her arm.

"Very well," he ground out, his jaw tight as he fought for control. "Perhaps I'll see you later? There's another assembly this evening. Will you ride with us in our carriage?"

Rose had planned to attend the assembly, but now the thought of watching Henry dance with Lady Dumfries turned her stomach. No, she couldn't bear it. "I'm afraid not," she replied coolly, lifting her chin. "There's too much to be done with the guests arriving tomorrow. But I'm sure you and the others will have a wonderful time."

Her words, spoken in that cool, precise tone, hit Henry like a punch to the gut. For a fleeting moment, he was transported back to his first season in London, when another woman had made him feel unwanted, like an inconvenience. Only this time, it wasn't just his pride that suffered—it was his heart.

He swallowed down the sting of her dismissal, forcing himself to face the truth. He loved her. The realization crashed over him with devastating force. The feelings he'd once harbored for Carla were nothing compared to the depth of what he felt for Rose. He wanted to marry her, to make her his in every way, to spend the rest of his life showing her just how much she meant to him. But if she didn't return his feelings—if she didn't love him—then he had no choice but to keep his distance.

Somehow, he would have to learn to live with that heartbreak.

Over the next few days, Rose kept herself busy, trying in vain to ignore the sad state of her heart. Between the endless dinner parties, picnics, and countless hands of cards, she saw very little of Henry. It seemed they had reached an unspoken agreement to avoid one another, a situation made all the easier by the crush of guests and activities that demanded their attention. She told herself it was for the best, yet memories of their shared closeness would creep in, and with them, a wave of mourning—for what had been, and what could have been.

Complicating matters further was the letter she had received from her great-aunt, inviting her to join her in Scotland. The old countess, it seemed, had finally decided to forgive her "black sheep" niece for her many failings and was now demanding Rose's presence at her side. Rose had told no one of the missive, keeping the knowledge tucked away like a secret escape route. It was the perfect excuse to leave Thornfield, should things with Henry become unbearable. But the thought of leaving filled her with equal parts relief and sorrow.

Deception, she thought with a weary sigh. Would the duplicity ever end?

The afternoon before the masquerade ball was surprisingly peaceful. Most of the guests were resting in preparation for the evening's festivities, and Rose, eager for a moment of solitude, decided to go for a ride. It was a pleasure she hadn't indulged in since the ill-fated trip to Derby, and as she rode across the green, rolling hills, she felt the quiet sadness of farewell settle in her chest. She knew, with a bittersweet certainty, that she was saying goodbye—not just to the land she had grown to love, but to the man who owned it.

As she reached the crest of a hill, she drew her horse to a stop, tears filling her eyes as she gazed out over the familiar landscape. She would always carry the memory of this place in her heart, and the memory of Henry would be there, too, a constant ache she would never fully be rid of. The thought brought a rueful smile to her lips. Finally, she mused, she was behaving like a true romantic heroine—starry-eyed and hopelessly in love.

On impulse, she nudged her horse toward the ruins, wanting one last visit before she left. But as she approached, she caught sight of a familiar figure standing among the stones. Henry. And beside him, Lady Dumfries.

Even as she registered the painful sight, she saw the marchioness fling her arms around him and draw him down into a passionate kiss. The sight was too much to bear. Rose's breath caught in her throat, and without a second thought, she wheeled her horse around and galloped away, tears streaming down her cheeks, her heart breaking with every beat.

Back at the ruins, Henry drew back from the kiss, his expression hard. "Really, Henry," Lady Dumfries said, her tone one of reproach as she gazed up at him. "You disappoint me. I thought we understood each other."

"Did we?" he asked, his voice cold as he studied her. He had brought her here on purpose, determined to face the demons of his past and put them behind him once and for all. It had been a test, and one he had passed with flying colors.

"I told you," she continued, a note of desperation creeping into her voice, "the choice wasn't mine. My parents insisted I marry Dumfries. What else could I have done?"

"Nothing."

The bluntness of his reply made her blink in surprise. "I wanted to accept you," she pressed, laying a hand on his arm and gazing up at him with what she no doubt thought was genuine longing. "You can't imagine how painful it was to send you away. My heart was breaking, but Mama was adamant."

"Now *you* disappoint me, Lady Dumfries," Henry said, his mouth twisting in a grim smile. "But you're mistaken if you think I hold your rejection of my suit against you."

Her eyes widened, and for a moment, she seemed unsure whether to be relieved or insulted. "You don't?"

"In fact, I've never been more grateful," he said, the satisfaction in his voice unmistakable. "Meeting you again has only confirmed what I've long suspected. Every night, I've been on my knees, thanking the Almighty for my deliverance."

Her face flushed an unbecoming shade of red, and without warning, she lashed out, striking him across the face with her gloved hand. "Bastard," she hissed, her voice trembling with fury. "You're as beastly and uncivilized as you always were."

Henry only chuckled, giving her a mocking bow. "Thank you, my lady," he said smoothly. "Fortunately, there's a certain woman who appreciates men who are beastly and uncivilized. Now, if you're quite finished attempting to seduce me, I think it's time we headed back. I've much to do."

Without waiting for a reply, he turned on his heel and strode back to his horse, leaving Lady Dumfries seething behind him.

Chapter Twenty-One

"Well, you look a sight, I must say," Maggie muttered, hands on her hips as she studied Rose. "Did the ladies really wear such queer things?"

"According to Lady Beatrice, they were all the rage some sixty years ago, although heaven knows how the poor creatures managed to fit through doorways," Rose replied, her expression dubious as she studied her reflection in the glass. "I look like a table that's decided to go exploring on its own."

The gown, designed in rich red brocade and lavishly embroidered with gold and silver threads, was a far cry from the modest and fashionable dresses Rose typically wore. Instead of the straight, graceful skirts she was accustomed to, the skirts of this ball gown extended a full sixteen inches on either side, making walking difficult and the thought of dancing laughable. The gown was also scandalously low-cut, and Rose was considering whether or not she should stuff another lace fichu into the neckline when Maggie spoke again.

"Mayhap it wouldn't look so odd if you was to wear one of them powdered wigs," Maggie suggested, eyeing Rose's attire thoughtfully. "I remember a grand lady from my village used to wear one, and I thought she looked like a queen."

Rose suppressed a shudder at the memory of the graying, vermin-infested wig she had found along with the gowns. "No, thank you, Maggie," she said, giving in to the desire for modesty and tucking the black fichu firmly into the tight bodice. "I shall be uncomfortable enough as it is, and I doubt Great-Aunt would thank me if I arrived at her home infested with fleas."

The mention of the countess and the impending move to Scotland made Maggie sniff in disapproval. "Don't know why we need to go tearing off to her ladyship's," she grumbled, moving behind Rose to finish arranging her hair. "What's wrong with this place, I'd like to know?"

Rose closed her eyes, the image of Henry kissing Lady Dumfries flashing before her once again. "Nothing," she said at last, her tone bleak as she opened her eyes to gaze into the mirror. "Only that it isn't our home, and we mustn't impose on his lordship's kindness any longer. Now that Lady Ashbourne has recovered from her injury, there's no reason to remain."

"Isn't there?" Maggie's expression turned secretive. "If you say so, Miss Rose, but I do wish you would reconsider; only remember what happened last time you went calling on your great-aunt."

Rose did remember, and it was all she could do to keep from bursting into tears. "It's different this time," she insisted, swallowing the lump that had risen in her throat. "Great-Aunt Charlotte has invited me, and you needn't make it sound as if we're sneaking off in the night like thieves. I fully intend to inform Lady Ashbourne of my decision tomorrow morning."

"And when do you plan to leave?" Maggie pressed.

"By week's end," Rose replied, giving her reflection one last glance before turning away. "That should give you enough time to pack, shouldn't it?"

Maggie handed her the ornate fan that completed the ensemble. "Oh, more than enough time, miss," she said with a cheeky grin. "More than enough."

The grand ballroom at Thornfield Manor had been transformed into a fairy woodland. After making her cautious way down the stairs, Rose paused to admire the result of her hard work. Blankets of white roses and ferns from the countess's greenhouse were interspersed throughout the room, mingling with delicate gilt chairs and tables. She had to admit the effect was enchanting.

"There you are," came a familiar voice, and Rose turned to find Henry standing behind her. The sight of him dressed as a Roman centurion made her breath catch. She gazed at him in amazement, her heart stuttering.

The expression on her face caused Henry to flush slightly with embarrassment. He'd felt like a fool, rigging himself out like this, but his mother had insisted on the costume. Given the alternative—a toga and olive-leaf headdress—he'd thought this was the better choice, but now he wasn't so sure. When Rose continued staring at him, he shifted uneasily from one sandaled foot to the other.

"I wish you'd say something, Rose," he muttered, striving for a light tone. "These things are damned uncomfortable, you know."

"No more uncomfortable than this," Rose replied, deciding that if he could act nonchalant, so could she. "At least you can move without knocking over everything in sight."

He took in her elaborate gown with its massive skirts and repressed a grin. "Actually, I think you look rather charming," he drawled, his eyes drifting to the neckline of her gown where she had tucked the lace fichu. "Although I think you could dispense with this," he added, running the tip of his finger along the lace. "Afraid of catching a chill?"

Her cheeks flushed, and she rapped his hand with her fan. "It's interesting, don't you agree, how many of our guests have chosen costumes that reflect their true selves?" she asked, her tone brisk as she attempted to steer the conversation away from his audacity. "Look at Mr. Langford, rigged out like a brigand, and there's Lady Langwicke dressed as Queen Bess. I always thought her far too regal for a mere marchioness."

Henry heard the nervousness beneath her chatter and wondered what was troubling her. Now that he had put his past to rest, he was ready to focus on his future, and he prayed she would be a part of it. Taking a deep breath for courage, he reached for her hand. "Rose, there's something I need to ask—"

"Speaking of marchionesses, will Lady Dumfries be coming?" Rose interrupted, her smile bright but brittle. "I'm sure her costume will be... most interesting."

"Carla?" Henry frowned at the sudden shift. "What makes you think she's coming tonight?"

"I..." Rose's voice faltered, and she stared at him for a long moment. "I assumed you had invited her, my lord," she said, ruthlessly smothering the small flicker of hope that had been kindled in her. "You've been spending a great deal of time with her lately and—"

"There you two are!" Lady Beatrice's voice rang out as she limped across the room to join them. "I've been looking for you everywhere." She fixed Rose with a pointed stare. "And what's this I hear about you going to Aberdeen? A fine notion of gratitude you have, to go sneaking off the moment my back is turned."

Rose felt the blood drain from her face, and then rush back just as quickly. She realized Maggie must have confided in Mabel, and Mabel, of course, had gone straight to Lady Beatrice. The private word Rose had hoped to have with the countess was now impossible, and aware that they were the object of several interested stares, she strove to maintain her dignity.

"I hadn't meant to abuse your hospitality, my lady," she said, speaking with all the decorum her father would have wished for. "But my great-aunt has written, requesting that I join her in Scotland, and I—"

"Scotland!" Henry's roar threatened to shatter the panes of the French doors. "If you think you're going to Scotland, you're out of your bloody mind!"

His harsh words brought an immediate hush to the room, and the fierce expression on his face caused several young ladies to swoon. Above the murmur of the crowd, Henry could hear someone muttering about "the beast," but he paid it no mind. Instead, he advanced on Rose, his hands clenched into fists.

"I have been patient long enough," he growled, his voice taut with emotion. "I told myself I would wait until I knew what you felt for me, but I can't hold back anymore. You're going to marry me, Rose, and that's the end of it."

Gasps echoed around them, followed by more swooning, but Rose barely registered it. Panic welled inside her. Could she trust him? Was he proposing out of love, or because he was piqued with Lady Dumfries? The thought of being his second choice—of being hurt again—was unbearable. She lifted her chin, her scowl fierce.

"As if I would marry an overbearing tyrant like you!" she declared, her voice trembling with emotion. "And even if I were foolish enough to overlook your barbaric manners, I would never condone your rakish ways!"

Henry had been called many things in his life, but never a rake. He blinked, momentarily at a loss. When no retort came to mind, he impatiently waved her accusations aside. "Rake or not, I will marry you," he said, grabbing her hand. "Now stop complaining and come with me. We have a wedding to plan." And before she could object further, he dragged her unceremoniously from the ballroom.

Rose fought against him, but with her cumbersome skirts and Henry's determined grip, it was futile. Once they were out on the balcony, he let her go. She wasted no time in swinging her fist at his face, but he dodged the blow easily, catching her hand and pulling her against him. His mouth came down on hers in a searing kiss, and at his touch, the fight drained out of her. Her hands clutched his shoulders, pulling him closer.

"Rose," he whispered against her lips, his voice low and urgent. "I love you. How could you ever think of leaving me?"

The husky words made Rose's knees go weak, and had Henry not been holding her so securely, she would have collapsed.

"You... you love me?" she asked, her eyes wide as she searched his face. "Are you sure?"

"Of course I'm sure," he replied with a husky laugh, the disbelief in her voice filling him with both joy and relief. He kissed her again, his lips brushing against hers before he drew back slightly.

"And now," he murmured, his hand toying with the lace fichu at her neckline, "don't you think it's time you told me you love me, too?"

She sighed under his touch, surrendering at last. "I do love you," she confessed, then spoiled her moment of submission by adding, "Although heaven knows why. You're a beast."

He grinned, recalling the sting of those same words in the past. "So I am," he agreed, his tone teasing. "And you are the least ladylike woman I've ever met. Can you think of two people better suited to one another?"

Rose considered that for a moment before breaking into a soft laugh. "No, I cannot," she admitted, linking her arms around his neck as she smiled up at him. "But before we get carried away, perhaps you can explain why you were kissing Lady Dumfries this afternoon. If you think I'll tolerate such behavior once we're married, you may think again."

Henry laughed at her stern tone, bending to kiss her sulky mouth. As he explained his need to finally put his childish infatuation with Carla behind him, he wasn't surprised that Rose understood completely.

"I only wish I had made similar peace with my father," she sighed, resting her head against his shoulder. "He was always berating me for my lack of ladylike qualities, but I think perhaps he would be proud of me now."

"I'm sure he was always proud of you," Henry said softly. "I think it's the way of parents and children to quarrel. Besides"—he lifted her chin and gazed into her eyes—"had you been ladylike, we might never have ended up here."

"That's true," Rose agreed, grinning as she remembered the bed warmer incident. But when Henry leaned in to kiss her again, she pulled back, eyes narrowed.

"Just let that be a warning, my lord," she cautioned. "Chase another pretty blonde into a bedchamber, and I'll do more than dent a bed warmer over your head. I trust I've made myself clear?"

"Quite clear, love," Henry said solemnly. Then, with mock frustration, he added, "Now I see why these damned side skirts went out of style." He scowled at the voluminous fabric that kept them apart.

"No gentleman of my grandfather's time would have tolerated such nonsense."

Their laughter was cut short when Lady Beatrice appeared, her eyes gleaming with satisfaction. "If you two have finished causing the scandal of the season," she drawled, "perhaps you'll return to the ballroom and announce your engagement? And do straighten your clothing—I'll not have people counting on their fingers when your son makes his appearance."

Both Henry and Rose blushed at such frank talk, but they quickly followed Lady Beatrice's instructions. They were almost at the ballroom doors when Henry suddenly chuckled and pulled Rose to a halt.

"What is it?" she asked, gazing up at him, her heart so full of love she feared it might burst.

"I was just thinking about your comment on costumes," he said, nodding toward his mother's retreating figure. "Do you not see how my mother is dressed?"

Rose frowned. "Like a Grecian lady, I suppose," she said, unable to see his point. "But I—"

"Like the Oracle of Delphi," he corrected, laughing as realization dawned. "All-knowing, all-seeing, and cleverer than all of us combined. Don't you see, my love? The wily old witch has outsmarted us all."

"And do you mind?" Rose asked, recalling the countess's scheming.

"Not in the least," Henry replied, bending to kiss her again. "As long as I have you, nothing else matters."

With that, they walked back into the ballroom together, the beast and his rose, their love sealed by laughter and a kiss—scandalous whispers be damned.

Epilogue

Rose stood before the mirror in her dressing room, her fingers tracing the intricate lace of her nightgown. The candles flickered, casting a warm glow over her flushed skin. Her heart fluttered with a mixture of anticipation and nervousness she hadn't felt since the night at the masquerade ball a fortnight ago.

"Who would have thought," she mused aloud, a small smile playing on her lips, "that a bed warmer could lead to this?"

The door opened quietly, and Henry's reflection appeared behind her. His eyes, dark with desire, met hers in the mirror.

"Having second thoughts, my love?" he teased, his voice low and husky.

Rose turned, raising an eyebrow. "About marrying a beast? Never."

Henry chuckled, closing the distance between them. "Then perhaps you're reconsidering your decision to tame said beast?"

"Oh, I wouldn't dream of it," Rose replied, her breath catching as he traced a finger along her collarbone. "Where would be the fun in that?"

Rose's arms wrapped around his neck, pulling him closer as she lost herself in the taste and feel of him. Every touch, every kiss, stirred a longing deep within her that she couldn't deny.

Henry's hand cupped her cheek, and Rose leaned into his touch, her eyes fluttering closed.

Their lips collided in a fiery fusion, their mouths hungry and insatiable. Rose's hands trembled as she desperately struggled to unbutton Henry's shirt, her fingers fumbling against the fabric. But he broke away, a wicked grin playing on his lips as he watched her struggle. The heat between them was palpable, igniting fervent desire and unleashing a tempestuous passion that could not be contained.

"Impatient, are we?"

"Insufferable man," Rose muttered, but there was no heat in her words.

Together, they slowly undressed each other, each newly revealed inch of skin explored with reverent touches and tender kisses. Rose's breath caught in her throat as Henry trailed his lips along the curve of her neck, his hands roaming over her body, igniting a fiery desire within her.

When at last they stood bare before one another, Henry gathered Rose in his arms and carried her to the bed. She lay beneath him, her body trembling with anticipation as he leaned down to kiss her deeply. His touch was like fire against her skin, sending waves of pleasure coursing through her veins.

"You're trembling," he murmured, concern furrowing his brow.

Rose smiled up at him, her hand caressing his cheek. "With love," she assured him. "With want."

Rose welcomed Henry's kiss as he lowered himself onto her, their lips locking in a sensual dance that sent shivers down her spine. She felt his growing arousal against her and arched her hips slightly in invitation. He accepted, pushing into her slowly, filling her inch by exquisite inch. Every move he made was matched by an equally delicious sensation: the brush of his warm skin against hers, the moan that escaped him as he buried himself deeper inside, the way he looked down at her with such raw desire and vulnerability that took her breath away.

Her fingers tangled in his hair as she wrapped her legs around his waist, drawing him closer still. His muscular frame trembled with effort as he held most of his weight off of her, giving them both time to adjust to the new sensation. The room filled with the sound of whispered endearments and soft sighs of pleasure. Rose marveled at how perfectly they fit together, how every touch, every caress seemed to ignite a fire within her.

In the aftermath, they lay entwined, their heartbeats slowly returning to normal. Henry's fingers traced lazy patterns on Rose's back, while she rested her head on his chest, listening to the steady thrum of his heart.

"A penny for your thoughts, my love," Henry murmured, pressing a kiss to the top of her head.

Rose propped herself up on an elbow, her eyes meeting his. With a soft smile, she took his hand and placed it on her belly. "I was just wondering," she said, her voice barely above a whisper, "if we've started our family this night."

Henry's smile split his face and he beamed at her. "A beautiful dark-haired, fiery tempered, daughter," he said. "Just like her mother."

"Or—" Rose fixed him with a steely look. "Look who is calling who fiery tempered! Heaven help our little boy if he's anything like his father!"

Henry laughed, and pulled her close, capturing her lips in a kiss that spoke of love, hope, and promises for the future.

As they settled back into each other's arms, Henry reached out to tuck a stray curl behind Rose's ear, just as he had done on that first night they'd waltzed together.

"I love you, my Rose," he whispered.

"And I you, husband."

"Beast and all?"

Rose smiled, snuggling closer. "Beast and all," she confirmed. "Always."

Here, in the arms of her beastly earl, she had found her happily ever after. And it was only the beginning.

About Violet Sinclair

Violet Sinclair is your passport to a bygone era of passion and extravagance. With an insatiable love for history, she dives headfirst into the world of ballrooms, lavish gowns, and Regency England. When she's not jet-setting with her adventurous sons, you'll find her indulging in her true passion: crafting sultry tales of love and desire, all while basking beneath the Florida palm trees. Step into her world, where every word is a whispered secret and every story a tantalizing journey into romance's heart.

https://violetsinclairromance.com/

Also by Violet Sinclair

The Duchess Diaries Series

Awakening Wicked – Book 1

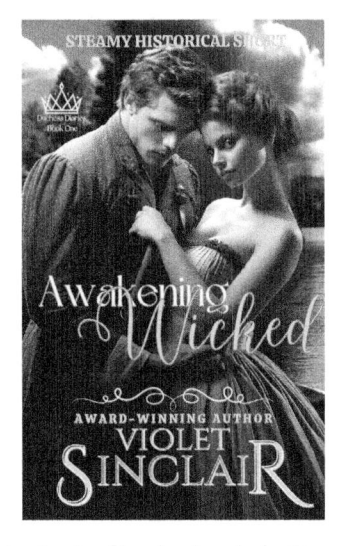

One year after the death of her husband, the Dowager Duchess of Devonshire gladly shed her mourning clothes. At six and twenty, Lilly is one of the richest and most influential young women of the ton. And quite possibly the most innocent of the widows. Finally free from her horrid marriage, one devoid of love, tenderness, and any kind of pleasure, the last thing Lilly longs for is the company of gentlemen. Determined to show Lilly all the joys of being a widow, her oldest and dearest friend, Lady Anne, convinces Lilly to join her for the weekend at the Rycroft's infamous house party in Surrey. A weekend that promises to awaken a passion Lilly knows lays buried deep inside her. A desire that will put Lilly on her way to becoming one of the ton's most wicked widows.

The stage is set. The players are in place. What or whom will be next on Lilly's list of awakening?

Wicked Widows Club – Book 2

The dowager Duchess of Devonshire's return to London high society is a fabulous one indeed when she accepts an invitation from Lady Pettiford to join an exclusive club of free women. The old countess runs the secretive Lady's Side, hidden behind the walls of the famed Whitterfield's gaming hell. Here the widowed women of the ton are free to pursue every pleasure—with their money, their desires, and most importantly—their bodies.

London's season of royal splendor and hidden debauchery is beginning. The ladies and gentlemen of the ton are flooding into town eager to mingle and posture, for gossip and scandal. Debutantes prepare to preen and attract proper husbands. And the Duchess has an agenda of her own. Awakened to her sensuality and sexual cravings, Lilly boldly explores new sensations and lustful fantasies in the pursuit of fulfilling her wicked list.

Wicked Wager – Book 3

In this third tantalizing installment of the Duchess Diaries Series, the audacious Lilly, the dowager Duchess of Devonshire, and Lady Anne embark on a daring game. The stakes are as scintillating as they are shocking.

The young and innocent Lady Jane has entered the scene. Intent on saving her from the potentially harsh realities of the marriage market, Lilly and Anne devise a cunning plan. They will test the mettle of Jane's suitors in a way only they can – through seduction. Each dalliance becomes a litmus test to eliminate unsuitable candidates and protect Jane from an ill-suited match. And an opportunity for these gorgeous widows to tally more gents off their scandalous lists and fulfill their wicked wager.

The Art of Being Wicked – Book Four

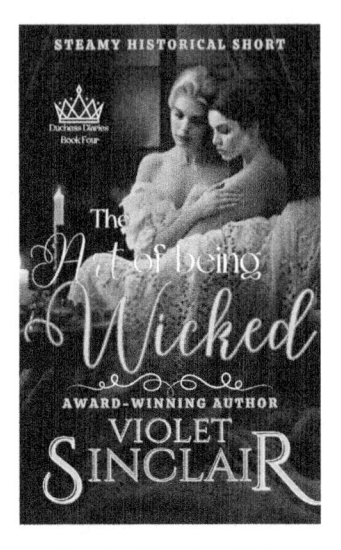

Behind the glittering façade of London high society, repressed passions smolder. When recently widowed Lilly, Dowager Duchess of Devonshire, receives a scandalous invitation, she's tempted to indulge her forbidden desires. But in this provocative world of illicit art and masked balls, embracing sensual freedom comes at a high price.

As Lilly's wanton adventures entangle her with her dearest friend and a seductive artist, she discovers that true liberation lies not only in unbridled pleasure, but in daring to be her authentic self.

A Hauntingly Wicked Eve – Book Five

When the enigmatic Marquess Blackthorn sends Lilly, the daring Duchess of Devonshire, an invitation to his notorious All Hallow's Eve masquerade ball, she cannot resist the lure of an evening cloaked in mystery and decadence. Venturing to the shadowy Ravenswood Hall with her trusted friend Lady Anne, Lilly finds herself caught up in a dizzying night of dark delights and unrestrained passion. But as ghostly whispers swirl through the manor's haunted halls, she begins to realize there are more secrets between these walls than she ever imagined.

After a passionate encounter with the Marchioness Blackthorn, Lilly becomes enthralled by a seductive masked stranger whose touch ignites her body like fire. She knows she should resist, yet cannot help surrendering to the raw, primal desire that consumes her. But is he truly flesh and blood, or something far more dangerous? Trapped in a dizzying world of illusion and sin, Lilly must navigate the tangled passions of the living and the dead if she hopes to uncover the truth.

With shocking twists that will leave you breathless, A Hauntingly Wicked Eve is an erotic story alive with thrills and temptation. Let Violet Sinclair sweep you into the haunting, decadent world of the Duchess Diaries once more.

Uncover their sordid adventures and unexpected discoveries in a world where pleasure and propriety collide. The rules of society are about to be rewritten, and every reader will want an invitation to this ball.

A Very Wicked Highland Christmas – Book Six

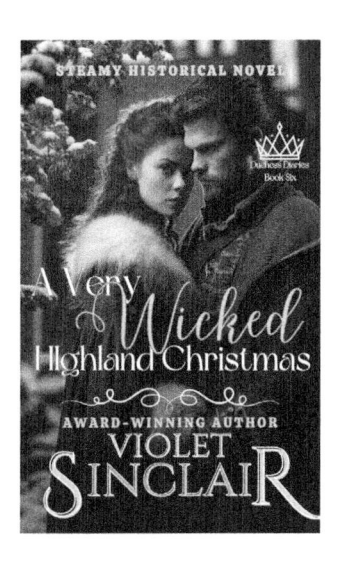

Join Lilly as she discovers love, passion, and her true self in the enchanting halls of Glenmoor Castle this holiday season.

When hearts are as wild as the Highland winds, love knows no season.

This Christmas, Lilly's return to Glenmoor Castle is about more than holiday cheer—it's about seduction, secrets, and a second chance with the earl who still haunts her dreams.

Lilly never imagined that her widowhood would be filled with such... wicked intentions. With a list of suitors from her past to tempt and tease, she arrives at the frost-kissed Glenmoor Castle for a Christmas she won't soon forget.

Graham, Earl of Crawford, is a laird bound by duty but yearning for love lost. When Lilly, the woman who once chose a title over his heart, reappears, their past passion reignites with the flicker of the Yule log.

As the Highland cold sets in, the warmth of newfound love blossoms, yet, with every stolen kiss, secrets of the past threaten to tear them apart. Can the magic of Christmas and the spirit of the Highlands heal old wounds and guide Lilly and Graham to a love that endures?

Step into the sixth installment of the Duchess Diaries, "A Very Wicked Highland Christmas," where the festivities are as intoxicating as the desire, and the spirit of the season may just bring the gift of love for those brave enough to unwrap it. Dive into the pages of this sizzling historical romance, where passion burns brighter than the Yuletide fires and love is as unpredictable as a Scottish storm.

The Lady's Side Series

Silk & Discretion – Book One

In the glittering world of Regency London, where whispers behind silk fans and closed doors can make or break a reputation, Lady Anne Hayworth finds herself at a crossroads. Widowed and longing for independence in a society that prizes male dominance, Anne's life takes a thrilling turn when she is introduced to The Lady's Side Club—a secret haven for the elite women of London.

"Silk & Discretion" is the first book in the captivating "The Lady's Side" series, where hidden desires meet daring actions. Within the walls of this exclusive club, Lady Anne discovers a world where women defy convention and embrace their desires, free from the constraints of societal expectations.

Haunted by the shadows of her abusive marriage, Anne's journey to self-discovery is anything but easy. As she navigates the treacherous waters of high society, she must also confront her own fears and desires. When she crosses paths with Arthur Crowley, a man of mystery with his own scars, Anne finds herself drawn into a passionate awakening that promises liberation and love.

But with her newfound freedom comes danger. Rumors and deceit swirl around Anne, threatening to ruin her reputation and her newfound sanctuary. Armed with her wit, the support of the fiercely loyal women of The Lady's Side Club, and the unexpected affection of Mr. Crowley, Anne takes a stand for her future.

From the opulent ballrooms of the ton to the intimate gatherings of The Lady's Side Club, Anne's story is one of courage, passion, and the quest for true independence. "Silk & Discretion" weaves a tale of sensual discovery, empowering friendships, and the unyielding strength of a woman determined to write her own story.

As alliances are forged and secrets revealed, Lady Anne Hayworth emerges as a beacon of hope and a trailblazer for women daring to challenge the status quo. Will she succeed in reclaiming her life and securing her heart's desires, or will the weight of scandal and society's expectations prove too much?

Her Viscount's Secret

In Regency-era England, Jane Seymour dreams of publishing her illustrations of rare birds, but societal expectations threaten to clip her wings. Enter Sebastian Westwood, the brooding Viscount with secrets as dark as his estate's shadowy corridors. When circumstances force them into a marriage neither expected, Jane and Sebastian must navigate a landscape of half-truths and hidden passions.

As Jane works to complete her magnum opus in the newly built aviary, she finds herself falling for the complex man behind the Viscount's mask. But Sebastian's past threatens to unravel their budding romance. With Anabelle, Sebastian's young ward, caught in the middle, Jane must decide if love is worth the risk of a broken heart.

Amidst the fluttering of rare birds and the rustle of sketch papers, can Jane and Sebastian build a love strong enough to weather any storm? Or will the secrets of Westwood Manor tear them apart?

"Her Viscount's Secret" is a sweeping Regency romance that will captivate fans of Julia Quinn and Lisa Kleypas. With its unique blend of artistic passion, family secrets, and tender romance, this novel proves that sometimes, love is the rarest bird of all.

Seductive Secrets and Regency Romance

Indulge in the world of passion, intrigue, and desire as you join Violet Sinclair's exclusive email subscriber list. Are you ready to immerse yourself in the tantalizing embrace of Regency romance?

Don't Miss Out on This Exclusive Journey!
CLICK HERE TO JOIN MY MAILING LIST:
https://subscribepage.io/SNJepq
You won't be spammed and can unsubscribe at any time

Printed in Great Britain
by Amazon